Tommy Green: Football is Magic

Simon Wellard

First published in 2023 by Fuzzy Flamingo
Copyright © Simon Wellard 2022

ISBN: 978-1-7391535-4-0

Editing and design by Fuzzy Flamingo
www.fuzzyflamingo.co.uk

A catalogue for this book is available from the British Library.

I would like to thank my family, especially Laura, Jamie and Reya, for all the love and support they have given me over the years. I would also like to thank Janna Walker for her counsel and David Joyner who introduced me to football coaching for the first time. Last, but by no means least, the hundreds of children who have given me so much fun and laughter in both my roles as a teacher and as a football coach. Thank you. This book is for you. Enjoy :0)

CHAPTER 1

The Gravity of the Situation

Sunlight streamed through the windows of class WD4T. Little Tommy Green stared out at the grass, desperately trying to ignore Mr Meener, his class teacher, who was currently standing on his desk, excitedly dropping pieces of screwed up paper and assorted heavy classroom objects onto the floor.

'Did you see that, children?' Mr Meener chirped. 'The stapler falls at exactly the same speed as the paper! How cool is gravity, hey?'

Tommy had to admit, it had been pretty cool the first three times, but now nine experiments in he was getting bored. What he would really like to see is Mr Meener being dropped off the school roof at the same time as a bit of paper. Now that would be a truly ace science lesson!

'Green! Are you paying attention, boy?' Mr Meener half bellowed, half shrieked across the room.

'Yes, sir, it was amazing, I really thought the stapler was going to win this time.'

Next to Tommy, Harry Smith tried unsuccessfully to stifle a snigger. Harry was Tommy's best friend. They had started school together when they were both four and had become mates immediately. Harry was much bigger than Tommy, but then to be fair most people were, even some of the year ones!

Riiiinnng

'Ah, saved by the bell, Green,' Mr Meener said. 'Now out to break, the lot of you, sensibly please.'

The break bell; Tommy's favourite sound. The class filed

1

out, pushing and shoving to get through the door all at once, but Tommy always managed to slip under someone's arm and be the first one out. Being small did have its advantages sometimes.

Harry and Tommy negotiated the winding corridors of Ridgeway Primary School out into the fresh air and made their daily pilgrimage up the stairs to the top playground. Both boys ran up them two at a time and stood at the top, taking in the sight of the hallowed concrete rectangle before them. The top playground was not just a playground for Tommy and his classmates, it was a gladiator pit with a battle of sporting football prowess against Robin Banks and the rest of the boys from class GO6L. A football match was staged almost every day and watched by an audience of junior class spectators. At one end, Mr Nomos the school caretaker had painted a white rectangle on the wall and at the other end a white rectangle on the fence. Harry took his birthday football out of the carrier bag his mum always made him carry it to school in and placed it on the painted centre circle. The ball was a replica of the one they'd used in the most recent World Cup and was Harry's pride and joy.

'How many do you think we will lose by today, Tommy?' Harry asked.

Tommy didn't answer, he was too busy watching a big mousey haired boy waltz over the playing fields with a 'celebrity' entourage following close behind.

'Oi, Green, you ready to get stuffed like a chicken?' Banks shouted as he approached. The other year six boys laughed.

'Banksy' was the school football captain. He had a head the size of an elephant's bottom and Tommy hated him almost as much as he wanted to be him. Robin Banks was very good at football. He had been spotted by an area scout and was playing for the county side as well as Bowden Park, one of the local town teams. Robin Banks. Everyone loved him; everyone but Tommy. Banksy picked on Tommy all the time. He would tell him he was rubbish at football, he was too small or too poor. It had all started when they had been playing football on the school field a couple of summers ago. Tommy had nutmegged Banks and then scored, but what had made it worse was Banks's mates had all teased him that a year two boy had made him look silly. Banks had singled Tommy out for revenge ever since.

The year six boys were all much bigger than Tommy's team of assembled year fours and fives, but he wouldn't swap any of them for the year six players. The year six boys always took the centre as well, even though it was Harry's ball. Banks passed the ball out wide to Owen Cash. Cash was a stick thin, gangly boy, but he had fantastic ball control with his left foot, and he was quick too. Cash took on the first year five and skipped around him before switching the ball to the other wing where a much stockier and stronger boy was waiting. Si Kling caught the ball on his chest and then volleyed it up the playground to their striker, Leon Mee. Mee jumped higher than Harry who was defending and headed the ball towards the fence goal. Terry Bull, who was playing keeper for Tommy's team, punched the ball up into the air. Tommy watched the flight of the ball carefully and got in line ready to kill it as it dropped onto his right foot.

'Mine!' came a big shout from behind Tommy. The next thing he knew, he was being knocked hard to the floor, just managing to see the ball fly past Terry and Banksy running off laughing.

'You're too small to play football, Green, you should give up and try a knitting class,' Banks announced to the whole playground. Laughter broke out all around as Harry leant down and hoisted his mate up to his feet.

'You all right, Tommy?' he asked.

'Yeah, I'm all right,' Tommy answered as he got to his feet

3

with a sense of Déjà vu. It would usually have been a clear foul, but the laws of the playground were very different.

That afternoon, Tommy sat with his head in his hands, watching the interactive whiteboard play a video about the Romans invading Britain. It seemed to Tommy that Julius Caesar had a similar problem. He kept trying to invade and beat Britain a bit like WD4T versus GO6L. In the end neither were quite good enough to win. Thirteen – six was the latest defeat. Robin Banks had scored three hat tricks and, each time he'd scored, he went up to Emma Nently and did a stupid dance that resembled an emu on roller skates. Emma would giggle and blush every time. This had made Tommy so cross. He liked Emma a lot, she lived next door to him, but she may as well have lived on the moon. She never seemed to notice him. Okay, she was a year older, but surely it wouldn't hurt to say hello once in a while.

'Thomas Green, are you listening?'

Grumpy Grimshaw, the afternoon cover teacher, was looking straight at him. She had obviously asked him a question, but he had no idea what it was. Sometimes you just have to be honest, put your hands up and say 'I wasn't listening, Miss', but not today; today Tommy tried the blag technique. It had to be something to do with Romans, didn't it?

'Eh, chariots, Miss?' he replied.

'So, you think that the Romans ate chariots, do you, Thomas?' Grimshaw scoffed. 'I suppose next you will tell me they covered them in tomato sauce to make them taste better!'

The class burst into laughter. Tommy turned a deep shade of red. He hated Grumpy Grimshaw; she always called him Thomas, as well! In fact, he didn't like school much at all. All he wanted to do was become a professional footballer. He was a good player but all the scouts who'd ever watched him had always said, 'He's a bit too small to be a real player.' What did they know?

4

After school that day, there was a football match scheduled against local rivals Thornside. Banks had been bragging about how Ridgeway couldn't lose because he was the best player in the town and he would destroy them all by himself. Tommy wished big mouth Banks would break a leg or something so he could get some peace. He and Harry climbed up the stairs to the top playground and walked across to the playing field. It looked perfect. Ridgeway was not a big primary school, but it had a lot of space and arguably the best football pitch in town. The school caretaker Mr Nomos took extra special care of the pitch because he loved football almost as much as Tommy. He'd grown up in Spain and would often chat to Tommy about the great Tiki Taka teams in the Spanish leagues he had idolised as a boy.

The emerald grass had been mown that very afternoon and the lines had been repainted such a brilliant white they could have been in an advert with an Old English Sheepdog. The red and black corner flags were brand new, donated by Banksy's dad, who owned Banks Electrical Engineering. They had a picture of an electric spark with a bumblebee in the middle, the company logo. To Tommy it looked like the bee had flown into one of those blue light thingies you see in chip shops. Mr Banks had donated a new kit as well, but no one had seen it yet. Tonight would be the first time it had been worn. The goals were top of the range Brazilian Beach Soccer Specials with custom red and black striped nets. Mr Point the PE teacher had got them through some sort of sports grant from a guy he knew that worked at a sports shop. I get a 20% discount he always bragged.

Tommy didn't really care about all that. He just longed for the day he would be allowed to thump a ball into the top corner and hear the net ripple. The nets were only ever used for matches, and he would probably have to wait at least another year before he could join the team. The very same team who were currently in Mr Point's classroom watching him scribble arrows and names all over his whiteboard until it looked like a bowl of spaghetti.

Parents, children and teachers were filling up on one side of the pitch ready to watch. The Thornside team was arriving in the car park, the familiar gold and blue shirts easy to spot.

'Do you reckon Neil Downe will be playing for Thornside tonight, Tom?' Harry asked lazily as they both took up their usual spot on top of the climbing frame.

Tommy put his coat over the bars, took out his juice bottle and balanced it carefully on the corner where two poles joined.

'Not sure, Hazza, I heard he twisted his ankle at training last Saturday.'

'Well, that's good for us then 'cause I think he's probably the best goalie I've ever seen.'

'Yeah, he is good,' agreed Tommy watching the Thornside boys start their warmup, 'but I don't see him yet.'

A small boy in a dark green shirt and royal blue shorts made his way over to the rest of the Thornside boys.

'Look, Hazza, Lee King is in goal, Neil must be out.' Tommy pointed towards the reserve keeper and then spotted an abnormally tall boy in a Thornside school uniform in amongst the crowd. Neil Downe. He lived on Tommy and Harry's street, but his mum taught at Thornside, so he went there instead of Ridgeway, which was actually closer. Tommy waved and Neil stuck up a huge arm that looked more like a flagpole above the now bustling crowd and waved back. Suddenly the familiar sound of Mr Point's CD player started to drift across the pitch. The voice of an overweight Italian man singing his heart out could be heard over the crowd and was followed by a line of marching red-and-black-shirted boys. Robin Banks at the front, hair immaculate, boots polished by his mum, CD player in his left hand, match ball under his right arm.

'I hate him, Haz.' Tommy scowled. 'I really do.'

'I know, Tommy, I know, but you've got to admit he is pretty good.'

'Mmmmhhh.' Tommy turned away so he couldn't see the farcical fanfare advancing towards him, just as the overweight Italian man sang a note that would have shattered Harry's glasses if they weren't made of plastic. Mr Point placed the match ball on the centre circle and blew the whistle, Banks and Markus Absent of Thornside shook hands and watched Mr Point toss the coin.

'Looks like Banks won the toss again,' Harry noted.

'Yeah, big surprise. The only thing I've ever heard him lose was a tooth!' Tommy said sarcastically.

After the game, Tommy trudged home, Harry at his heels, his carrier bag holding the precious World Cup ball over his shoulder. Tommy was reflecting on the game, replaying every kick, every throw-in, every run. Banks hadn't broken a leg, he'd scored four goals and set up two more. There would be no living with him tomorrow. His head would be so big that no one else would get into the school hall for the morning assembly.

'Cheer up, Tom, at least we won, mate,' geed up Harry, sensing his friend's frustration.

He understood why Tommy didn't like Robin Banks. It was hard not to be jealous of the boy who had everything you desperately wanted. Tommy loved football and wanted nothing more than to be a professional footballer. It must have hurt every time he heard the scouts say he was too small. The boys turned the corner into Granville Street and broke into their routine sprint to the third lamppost.

'I nearly beat you that time, Tommy, are you getting slower?' Harry jibed as he swung around the lamppost.

'I think you must be getting quicker, Haz, what have you

7

been eating?' Tommy laughed. The two boys grinned at each other, slightly doubled over, catching their breath. Tommy had deliberately run a little slower just to give Harry a bit of a morale boost and to make things interesting, but he would never admit that to Harry.

'See you tomorrow, Tommy.'

Harry carried on walking three houses further up the street as Tommy swung through his green garden gate. 'Green, get it?' his dad had said as he painted it two summers ago. That was before he'd died. He'd been in a car accident on his way back from work late one winter's evening. Worst snowstorm for forty years, the weatherman had said. It had been just over a year and a half since the accident and Tommy's mum had gone back to work full time at the local supermarket. He lifted the hessian mat and found the key for the big wooden door, let himself in and chucked his school bag and coat under the stairs. He raided the fridge for some juice and a couple of sausage rolls, remembering to get a plate for the crumbs. He made his way into the lounge and jumped onto the sofa. Using the TV remote, he quickly found the recorded episode of yesterday's football round up. The host introduced the panel of ex-professional players that Tommy's dad had promised him were great back in the day. The bald one had been his dad's favourite. 'Shot like a rocket!' he would always say. Tommy hit fast forward and got to the first game. He sat glued to the screen for the next fifty-two minutes, not noticing his mum arrive home. He found her in the kitchen later looking pensively at some letters that Tommy guessed were bills. She looked up as he entered and hastily bundled them into a drawer.

'Hiya, Mum, good day?' he chirped.

'Aye, not bad, pet. What do you want for yer tea?' She sighed.

'Have we got any fish fingers? I really like them.'

'Aye, pet, you want chips and beans as well?'

'Yes, please, Mum.'

He threw his arms round her waist and hugged her tight. Mrs Green ruffled her son's messy mop of jet-black hair and kissed the top of his head.

'Go get changed out of yer school clothes then, pet, and I'll put it on.'

Tommy ran up the stairs and opened the middle door of the three. His walls were completely full of posters he'd collected from his weekly football magazines. Not one inch of the wallpaper showed through. Tommy had even put a player over the light switch and then carefully cut around the square plastic case so that the white shirted centre forward now resembled a sort of children's TV character. His carpet was a very worn green and brown, but Tommy liked to pretend it was a football pitch. Using an assortment of action figures, other knick-knacks and his dad's old ping-pong ball, he'd recreate cool free kick routines he'd seen on the TV. He jumped onto his bed and lay back on the red bedspread gazing at all the famous faces staring back at him. Most of the wall was red for the team his whole family supported. He often wondered if his face would be on someone else's bedroom wall one day. He kicked off his shoes and pulled his diary out from under the mattress. He didn't let anyone see his diary, not even Harry! He found the correct date and began to write:

I hate Robin Banks [this is how most of his entries started]. Today we lost 13-6! Banks scored nine goals and Emma was loving it. I scored five but she didn't even look at me! Harry scored our other one. He's definitely getting better. Grumpy Grimshaw made me look stupid again today. Who cares what the Romans did for us 2000 years ago? Straight roads are boring, anyway. Can you imagine a rally driver being happy just driving straight? All I care about is what the Reds are going to do this Saturday. School won against Thornside 7-2; we were lucky Neil Downe couldn't play as he would never have let seven in. We are probably top of the league now, though, which is good, I suppose, but Banks will be a nightmare!

He finished his entry with a picture of Mr Meener racing a cricket ball off the school roof.

'Tea's ready, pet,' his mum called.

Tommy jumped off his bed and quickly shrugged off his school clothes. He skilfully flicked them with his foot into his football themed laundry basket. 'Goal!' he mimed, punching the air in front of his self-made kop end of famous faces in just his pants.

He rummaged through his drawers and found some shorts and a t-shirt with a World Cup logo on. He'd collected sixty-six drinks can ring pulls one summer to get it. Tommy had asked all his friends to save them for him and in return he had traded marbles, football stickers and plastic superheroes from his cereal boxes. He'd only just made the deadline. His mum had given him the money required for the postage and packaging and then they'd both taken his jangling parcel to the post office. That's when the agonising wait of the twenty-eight days for delivery had started. Twenty-eight days is a really long time when you're desperate for a t-shirt and only seven years old.

'Do you think it's got lost in the post, Mum?' he'd asked her almost every day. 'But what if one of the ring pulls falls out?' It hadn't and it eventually arrived. He smiled at himself in the mirror. It was a bit big still but that just meant he could wear it for longer.

'Tommy, it's getting cold!'
'Coming, Mum.'

CHAPTER 2

Trials and Tribulations

The next day Tommy was sitting in assembly next to Harry. Mr Binrite the headteacher was running through the usual weekly events. On Thursday, some dance troop was coming in to teach some of the other classes how to move like animals as part of their science project.

'It's YC3P, oh and BR2D too,' Mr Binrite informed them. 'And don't forget the PTA are having a cake sale on Saturday to raise money for the new trim trail in the reception playground.'

Tommy was half listening, half planning corner kick routines in his head for the breaktime battle, when suddenly his attention snapped straight back on to Mr Binrite.

'As you may know, children, there was a football match on last night against Thornside in which Ridgeway were victorious with a score of seven – two and this puts us at the top of the league on goal difference,' Mr Binrite beamed. 'Well done to those boys who played in last night's game, let's give them all a clap. What you may not know, however, is at the game there was also a United scout, and it gives me great pleasure to announce that our very own school captain Robin Banks has been selected for a trial at their academy next week. Stand up, lad, stand up.'

The school began to cheer and clap spontaneously as Banks beamed like a cat who had not only got the cream but had also packed four rare shiny cards in a single pack.

'Obviously we wish you all the best with the trial, Robin,' Mr Binrite continued.

Not all of us, thought Tommy.

During his English lesson, Tommy sat with his head in his hands. Why did Robin Banks have to be so good at everything? United! A jealous rage clouded all his thoughts. Just what would Banks be like if he got selected?!

'Tommy Green, have you finished?'

A tall, thin woman strode down between the row of tables and peered over Tommy's shoulder. Miss Alaynious, one of the school teaching assistants, was taking the class as Mr Meener was off work. His brain had probably exploded as he tried to think of more things to throw off his desk. She picked up his book and read the contents of his morning's work to the class in a posh accent that people usually reserve for answering the telephone.

'Thursday 14th of September. Adjectives. Jammy, slimy, lucky, stinky, muppet. I think it's safe to say, Mr Green [he hated it when she called him that], you won't be going out to break today. And, for future reference, muppet is a noun!'

Since Mr Binrite's big announcement in assembly, the whole school had been talking about Banks's United trial. The year six hangers-on had fallen over themselves to sit next to him at dinner, the girls had been sending him little notes asking him to marry them when he was famous, and the infants had been getting him to sign autographs! Banks was loving it, but for Tommy, it had been unbearable. He hadn't played football all week, partly because he had spent three breaktimes in detention and partly because he didn't want to see any more of Robin Banks than he had to. Harry had been just as bad as the rest of them cooing over Banks, asking him what boots he would wear if he became famous. Did he ever think he would play for England? England?! He hadn't even got into United yet. Tommy had avoided Harry too, which was why he was walking to school on his own. He rounded the corner onto Ridgeway Road and trudged towards the black school gates. Banks had been for his trial the day before, after school. Hopefully things would return to normal and Banks would have to admit he wasn't good enough because he'd not been selected.

Parents were dropping children off, giving final kisses and hugs and saying, 'have a nice day'. He negotiated the crowds and moped towards the top playground. With any luck, the bell would go, and he wouldn't have to speak to anyone. A large group of boys were in the centre, making a sort of uneven circle, Harry right in the thick of it. No prizes for guessing who was in the middle, Tommy thought.

'Did you see anyone famous?'

'What were the changing rooms like?'

'When do you find out if you're in?'

'One at a time, lads, one at a time. I have to go back now for another five weeks, then if I'm selected after that, I can sign a contract and be part of their academy.'

Five more weeks of this! Tommy turned quickly and tried to sneak away before being noticed.

'Oi, Green, don't you want an autograph?' Banks called out.

Tommy turned towards the circle of boys, which had now opened so that Banks was flanked on either side like he was performing on stage with a backing group choir, only instead of singing, they were sniggering. Tommy looked straight at Harry; Harry looked away quickly.

'Yeah, sure, why not? It might be worth something one day.' Tommy pulled a pen and a bit of paper out of his bag and walked towards him.

'Are you gonna frame it and put it on your wall?' Banks sneered.

'Nah, I was thinking I could sell it to the natural history museum as evidence that evolution may be true, after all.

People will queue up for miles to come and see the famous ape writing and I could give talks like the man off the TV does.' Tommy put on his best fake posh voice like he was a university professor. "Yes, I went to school with him, he even managed to tie his own shoelaces once and he nearly cut up his own food with a knife and fork without his mummy".'

Some boys tried to stifle sniggers; others just stood opened-mouthed in shock. Banks just glared at him. He might have been good at football, but Robin Banks was not so good at English. He had always struggled with his reading and writing. Everybody knew better than to say anything about it as, not only was Robin Banks a particularly good footballer, he also had a blue belt in karate. Banks walked towards Tommy menacingly, fists clenched by his sides. *This is gonna hurt*, Tommy thought. Banks lined up to thump Tommy in an over-exaggerated martial arts stance that was a cross between a flamingo-shaped hedge and someone desperate for the toilet, when suddenly Harry stepped in between them.

'Out of my way, Smith, this don't concern you,' Banks snarled.

'He's my best friend, so it does concern me,' Harry said proudly just as the bell went. He turned round to look at Tommy, hoping this would make them friends again, but Tommy was already walking into school.

'See you at breaktime, Green!' Banksy shouted.

Harry picked up his ball and chased after Tommy. He managed to catch up with him in the corridor. 'Tom, don't be mad with me, mate; I hate it when we don't get on. I was just interested to know what it was like. You understand that, don't you?'

'Yeah, I guess.' Tommy shrugged. He hoped Harry hadn't seen the tears in his eyes as he'd wiped his nose on his sleeve. 'Thanks for sticking up for me, Haz.'

They shook hands and went into class. Tommy wondered

15

what Mr Meener would have in store for them today that could put them both to sleep until breaktime. Apparently, Mr Meener was now feeling better after discovering goat yoga!

Tommy walked along the road after school, his head clouded in thought. He had missed both breaktime and lunchtime because of detention. He had deliberately got himself in trouble so that he could avoid a Banksy bashing. Tommy was not thinking about that now, though. A letter had come round at the end of the day inviting year fours to try out for the school team. Si Kling the school right winger had sprained his ankle jumping his BMX off a homemade ramp and was out for at least three weeks. With the school being so small, Mr Point had no choice but to look at his year fours to fill the gap for the next two league fixtures. What could he do? He wanted desperately to go to the after-school trials, but he had no boots. He couldn't turn up in just his school shoes or plimsoles, he would be a laughingstock. Visions of how he would show everybody what a great player he was soon took over. He imagined himself dribbling around the whole team and striking the ball into the back of the net. He then began to think about what celebration he should use. The robot? The shirt over your head? The floss? The full-length dive? Singing into the corner flag? Nah, he didn't like singing.

Tommy looked around him; the buildings didn't look familiar. A wave of panic started to wash over him. How far had he walked? He knew town pretty well but didn't recognise this street. There was a shop up on the corner, maybe he could go in and ask for directions. He ran quickly to the shop door and stopped abruptly at the bottom steps. A big dusty sign above the window caught his eye. "MR REE'S SPORTS MEMORABILIA". Football artefacts adorned the display area; old boots, photos, programmes, scarves, a whistle, a rattle, a brown leather ball, some odd-looking keeper gloves. *Wow*, thought Tommy, *how did I not know about this place?* He climbed the steps and pushed the old wooden door open slowly. A small bell chimed above him as the door creaked open into the store. Tommy closed the door and savoured all the delights that greeted him. It was the most wonderful place he had ever seen. It looked just like his grandad's shed with things hanging down from the ceiling and piles high on the floor, only it was full of sports things rather than old wellingtons and spades. It was surprisingly big inside too. From the outside, Tommy had expected a small shop with a counter and maybe one or two shelves, but the main counter was way at the back of the shop, almost the width of the school pitch away from the front door, and the corridors of shelves seemed to go off in all different directions. He couldn't even see the end of one long corridor to his left. Tommy was just trying to figure out the dimensions when a voice brought him to attention.

'Can I help you, young man?'

Tommy turned towards the voice and saw a small old man with glasses and a neat little moustache. He was wearing a fawn-coloured apron and a strange-looking red hat that looked like an upside-down bucket with a tassel on it. He was looking straight at him.

'I've got lost and was hoping you could tell me where I am,' Tommy said.

'Ah, wandered a bit too far, did you? Thinking about tomorrow's trial, no doubt,' the man replied.

How on earth does he know about the trials? Tommy thought.

'You're little Tommy Green, aren't you?' the man asked.

'Er, yes sir, how did you know?' Tommy replied.

'I knew your dad, lad, he was a good player in his day. I can see the resemblance. You look just like him. I bet you're as mad keen on football as he was.'

Tommy walked a little closer to the counter; the man seemed friendly enough.

'I have something here I think you might like,' said the man. He walked behind a thick purple curtain and returned with an old green tobacco tin. The man opened it carefully and inside there were some old football cards. They were bound together with a thick rubber band. He took off the band and started to shuffle through the pack. 'Ah, here they are. Do you know who these players are, Tommy?'

Tommy looked at the two cards in the man's hand. They were old but one was of a big man with a large moustache and, under the picture, it read "Alfred Openshaw". The other was of a foreign-looking man with black slicked-back hair, a little neatly trimmed beard and a blue shirt, smiling his head off. His name read "Antonio Rossi".

'No, sir, I'm afraid I don't.'

'They were both great players in their day. Alf was one of England's finest centre halves and Toni was one of the most skilful players to ever grace the game, but I am sure they will tell you that themselves.'

What a strange thing to say, Tommy thought, but he liked football cards and he was fairly sure no one else at school would have these ones. He could show Harry them tomorrow.

'How much are they?' Tommy asked eagerly.

'For you, my lad, they are free, my gift. Just promise you will come back and tell me how you got on with your trial tomorrow.'

The trial; Tommy had clean forgot.

'I don't think I'm going to try out,' Tommy said.

'Why ever not? You do like football, don't you?' the man asked.

'Yes, I do, I love it, but I have no boots, mine are broken and I don't think my mum can afford to buy me new ones at the minute.'

18

'Mmm, then you're in a bit of a pickle, aren't you?' The man rubbed his beard and disappeared behind the purple curtain once more. This time, he returned with an old brown shoe box. 'Here, these should fit,' he said. He blew the dust off the top of the box and fished out a pair of antique-looking boots. 'You can borrow them and bring them back when your trial is over.'

Oh no, they were really old, but the man had gone to so much trouble. Tommy forced a smile. 'Thanks,' he said.

'Now, we should really get you home, otherwise your mother will be worried sick. Follow me.'

Tommy tucked the shoe box under one arm, put the cards in his pocket and then followed the man down one of the many corridors of shelves. It bent to the left then to the right and then to the left again, it was almost as long as his street! Eventually, they came to a door. The man opened it and stepped to one side.

'Here you go, Tommy, I think you will recognise this street.'

Tommy stepped out onto what he recognised as Maurice Road. It was just two streets from his home. He turned back to thank the man for his help, but the back door of the shop had gone and now it was the door to someone's house. Where had the shop gone? Had he imagined it? He had the shoe box under his arm, so he couldn't have imagined it. He put his hand into his pocket and quickly pulled out the two cards. This was very strange. Tommy knocked on the door urgently. After a few minutes, an old lady opened it.

'Can I help you, love?' she asked.

'Um, is this the football shop?' Tommy quizzed the lady, already guessing the answer before she replied.

'Are you trying to be funny? It's not nice to pick on the elderly, you know.'

Tommy looked past her and could see some stairs and

a kitchen that were not there before. Confused and a little scared, he turned and ran away quickly for the safety of home.

CHAPTER 3
Card Tricks

Tommy lay on his bed trying to make some sense of the evening's events. He had drawn the strange shopkeeper in his diary earlier and hastily scribbled down all he could remember about the shop itself. He had asked his mum if she knew where it was, but she had never heard of a sports shop like it anywhere in the town, let alone a few streets away. 'It's just housing round here, pet,' she had said.

But he couldn't have imagined it because he had the old boots and the cards. How could that be explained? He took one of the boots out of the box and examined it. They were ancient. The old brown leather smelt fusty, and the laces had definitely seen better days. Inside the boot, there was a name written in black pen. It looked like it said S Martin. He would look ridiculous in these, but what choice did he have? Banks would have a field day. Tommy put his diary safely back under his mattress and got ready for bed. He closed his eyes tight, wishing for tomorrow to come faster.

The next day, it was so hard for Tommy to sit still. He'd hardly been able to sleep the night before with both a mixture of excitement and nerves in his stomach. He doodled on a bit of paper, a self-portrait of him wearing the Ridgeway red and black kit, dribbling a ball, with the old boots on. He was right, he would look ridiculous. He had sat in the library for both break and lunch, not wanting to go anywhere near Banksy, and now he was in his afternoon maths lesson.

'Thomas Green!' Grimshaw bellowed. 'Are you listening to me?'

The short answer was no, but that would probably get him yet another detention.

'Yes, Miss, of course, Miss,' he replied hastily.

'Good, so if you could kindly answer the question, then?'

Oh no, not again, he couldn't afford detention today, he needed to go to the trials. Tommy looked around the room sheepishly; maths was his worst subject. There was no clue on the board, or in Mrs Grimshaw's hands.

'Well? We're all waiting, Thomas.'

Just then, Tommy spotted something out of the corner of his eye. Harry had written the number thirty-two on his whiteboard and had propped it up at an angle so that Grimshaw couldn't see.

'Thirty-two,' Tommy blurted out.

'Thirty-two what?' she asked impatiently.

'Thirty-two, er… Miss?' Tommy replied.

'No, no, I mean pounds, percent, grams, what is the unit of measure?'

Grimshaw looked like she was about ready to explode. Tommy looked back over at Harry; this time he had drawn a large 'm' on his board.

'Oh, er, metres, Miss?' Tommy prayed this was the right answer and it wasn't miles.

'Yes, that's correct, Thomas, well done, wonders will never cease. Maybe you *were* listening, after all.'

Grimshaw turned around as Harry slipped his board quickly under his book. Tommy nodded over at Harry, who returned the gesture with a huge grin. *Close one*, thought Tommy. The bell went and Grimshaw dismissed the class. Tommy slipped through under the arm of Hugo Thurstden and into the corridor, Harry close behind him.

'Cheers, Haz, I owe you one.'

'No worries, you can give me that shiny you got in your football cards last week, that should cover it,' Harry joked.

'What, the Reds' own Captain Marvel? No chance!' Tommy laughed. 'I'd rather have detention than give you that! You know he's my hero.'

They crossed the playground and went into the pavilion. Although it had a posh sounding name, what it really was, was a concrete shell with some benches inside. No lights or heating and grubby breeze block walls meant it wasn't the best changing room in the world, but to Tommy it was all part of the magic. He put on his beloved Reds' replica kit with the large number eight on the back and then looked down at the old boots the strange little man had given him.

'Ha, what are them things, Green? Did you borrow them from your granny?' Robin Banks looked over, immaculate in his third set of new boots that season – and it wasn't even Christmas yet! 'Watch out there, might be mice living in them, bite yer toes off like.'

Banksy walked out flanked by school goalkeeper Liam Mackenzie – or Big Mac as everyone called him – and defender Rohan De Boat. Tommy could still hear them laughing from the field. He slipped the boots back into his bag and put on his plimsoles.

'It's all right, Tommy, just play well and get yourself in the team. That will shut Banksy up,' Harry said, trying to cheer him up.

Tommy looked up and forced a smile back at Harry. He was right, though, if he could get in the school team as a year four that would be something even Banksy hadn't managed to do, and Tommy would have the bragging rights.

Outside, the pitch looked amazing. The goals had on their plain nets as it was only a training night. The grass was littered with traffic cones and brightly coloured pitch markers, and some of the lads were doing keepy-uppies. Mr

Point was pumping up some footballs and Robin Banks was taking penalties against Big Mac. He never missed. Tommy stopped to watch as the school captain went through his daft routine of turning away from goal then spinning quickly and running to smash the ball into the net. Only... his angle was all wrong... this was never going in... could Robin Banks actually miss this one? Banks hammered the ball with his laces, only instead of aiming at the goal, he was aiming straight at Tommy. The ball flew through the air at full speed. Tommy ducked. If he hadn't been watching, it would have hit him for sure.

'Ahhhh!' A voice cried out in pain behind him. Tommy turned around to see Harry holding his nose, blood pouring through his fingers.

'Sorry, Smithy, I was aiming at your little mate, Green!' Banks called out. Only Banks didn't sound at all sincere. He just turned away and fetched another ball.

Tommy called out to Mr Point, 'Mr P [it was what he liked to be called], Harry has a nosebleed.'

Mr Point looked over. 'Okay, Tommy, take him down to the office, please.' Then he went back to pumping up the balls.

'Come on, Haz,' Tommy said with some guilt. After all, if he hadn't ducked out of the way, Harry wouldn't have got hit. He took the bigger boy by the elbow and led him down to the school office.

Tommy sat in the office reception area waiting for Mrs Flett the school secretary to clean up Harry. It would not have been right to go to the trial without Harry. Flipping Banks, why wouldn't he just leave him alone? It was because Tommy had ridiculed him in the playground; what had he been thinking, teasing him about his writing? He should have just walked away, but Banks always wound him up so much. He rolled down his sock and took out the cards, which he'd slipped in there whilst he was getting changed. He looked at big Alf, wondering how good he had been.

Woah! No way! Had the man on the card just winked at him? No, impossible. Tommy looked again, staring at Alf's face. Now he was smiling and waving at him. Tommy rubbed his eyes and looked again. It looked like he was now trying to speak to him. Tommy watched Alf's mouth carefully. 'How do, lad' he said in a thick Yorkshire accent.

Tommy shoved the cards back into his sock.

'Mamma Mia, who-a turnt outta the lights?' said another little voice; this time sounding Italian. This was not happening, surely.

Tommy was just about to get the cards out again when he heard, 'Tommy let's go!' Harry was beaming at him. 'Come on, there's still half an hour to go. It's time to show Banks what we can do.'

Tommy looked up quickly then back to his sock. Had he just imagined this as well? He needed to find the little shop again, somehow, and get some answers. For now, though, he followed Harry back onto the pitch with renewed energy.

A game was already under way. The school first team minus an injured Si Kling was facing a ragtag mix of year fives and fours that had all turned up for the trial. Mr Point was in the middle refereeing. He pointed to three children who were sitting down near the spare balls There were too many trialists and so some children were sitting on the bench – or the grass, as it actually was. Two year four boys, Artie Choak and Chris Tall, both veterans of the breaktime battles, and a new girl from year five.

'Hey, Tommy,' Chris called. 'Hazza.'

Tommy and Harry sat down next to him and Artie.

'Who's the new girl?' Tommy asked.

'Dunno, she transferred last week from some school in

25

London,' Fred replied. 'Laura Noarder told my sister she's a bit funny, like.'

Tommy looked over. 'Hey, I'm Tommy, what's your name?' The new girl looked over towards the boys.

'Bailey, swap with Edward, please.' The ball had gone out for a throw-in, and Mr P had decided to switch things about. 'Chris, swap with Dan, Artie and Harry swap with Philip and Justin, Tommy swap with Joe in goal.'

'But I don't play in goal, sir,' Tommy called out.

'Oh, okay, then, perhaps you would prefer to sit and watch,' Mr P replied sternly.

'No, sir, I will play in goal.' Tommy trudged into the only position on the pitch he didn't like to play. Being small meant he often couldn't reach the higher balls and so he couldn't save them. People would laugh at him and call him names like Titch and Shorty.

'Right, all sorted, play on, Robin.'

Banks threw the ball long from the right of Tommy's goal. Owen Cash controlled the ball with the outside of his left foot then flipped it quickly with the inside past Artie's outstretched foot, then in one swift movement flicked it back through Artie's legs with the outside of his left foot again.

'Megs!' he shouted as he zipped around the bewildered Artie.

Robin Banks had stolen a run down the wing on Tommy's left and was calling for it. Owen was shaping to pass the ball across the pitch straight into his path. *No, you don't,* Tommy thought and he started to move into the space to intercept the ball. *I might not be any good in goal, but I can run out and play on the pitch.* The ball was hit exactly where Tommy had predicted, no way Banks was getting this one.

'Tommy's!' he called.

'Bailey's!'

Tommy looked to his left, the new girl was running to

intercept the same ball and she was quick too. Bailey nipped in front of Tommy, took the pass on her chest, then span and played a quick pass into Chris's feet. Tommy watched open-mouthed as she sailed past Rohan De Boat. Chris hit a long ball into the space just in front of Mackenzie's goal area as Bailey raced through. Big Mac was off his line and trying to chase down the ball, but he wasn't quick enough. Bailey arrived at the ball first with at least two metres of space separating her and the onrushing keeper. She calmly knocked the ball past him on his left-hand side and ran around the other way on his right. Mackenzie's momentum meant he went rushing through the space between Bailey and the ball. Bailey met the ball on the other side and calmly passed it into the empty net.

'Well done, Bailey,' Mr P beamed at her.

'Thank you, sir,' she replied, smiling.

'Centre, the score is eight-one to the first team,' Mr Point reminded everyone.

'Eight-one with only six players! Tommy brooded. Banks took the centre with school forward Leon Mee. Mee knocked it back to Ally Gayter in defence. Ally Gayter was not quick, but he was very strong and could kick a ball the full length of the pitch. Banks and Leon sprinted down the centre, knowing Gayter would be hitting a long ball deep into the opposite half. *Whack!* The ball soared above the onrushing Bailey, over Chris and Wayne Dwops from year five in midfield and over Harry and Artie. Terry Bull, also from year five, was supposed to be playing left wing for the trial team but was doing up his laces by the touchline. All that stood between the goal, Banks and Leon was Tommy. Tommy rushed off his line quickly, but his right plimsole came off, making him slip. Banks trapped the incoming missile from Gayter with the inside of his right thigh. The ball dropped to his feet, and he looked up, just as Tommy went sprawling. Banks chipped the ball up and over the

stranded Tommy, who was now lying face down outside the penalty area. Leon Mee, who had continued running towards the empty goal, met the lofted ball with his head and it nestled in the bottom corner.

'B team centre, nine-one,' Mr P called out cheerily.

Terry, who had now tied his boot laces, passed the ball to the new girl, Bailey. Banks pounced and flew into her, completely missing the ball and knocking her over. It was obviously on purpose.

'Oops, sorry,' he sniggered, walking away, high-fiving with Leon as he did so.

'Free kick,' called out Mr Point.

Bailey put the ball on the halfway line. It was too far away to shoot, surely. She called Chris, Terry, Wayne and Harry over to her and they started to whisper in a little huddle. Artie started to walk towards them, but Bailey put up her hand and told him to stay back. Tommy was desperate to know what they were saying but he couldn't leave the goal. Terry was now doing up his other boot on the right wing. Tommy watched longingly as Bailey shaped up to kick the ball down the centre. Harry was standing behind her, Chris to her right and Wayne was next to the ball. Mr Point blew his whistle and Bailey made her run to the ball, she pulled back her leg to kick it but instead ran straight over the ball, just as Chris arrived and did exactly the same. Bailey was now running down the centre and Chris down the left. Wayne toe-poked the still stationary ball out to Terry Bull, who was unmarked because he'd been tying up his boot laces, or so everyone had thought. Terry jumped up and stopped the ball with the bottom of his foot. The first team players all rushed towards him, but he calmly stepped back just as Harry arrived, running full tilt, smashing the ball over the advancing year sixes down towards a now free Chris Tall. Chris had plenty of time and space to control the cross-field pass. He then dribbled quickly towards Liam Mackenzie's goal, drawing the keeper out to his right. Chris shaped to shoot but, instead, played the ball square to Bailey, just behind the penalty spot. Ally Gayter was the closest to her, snapping at her heels. He tried to slide tackle the ball away, but Bailey trapped the ball between her ankles and jumped with the ball still between her legs, over the sliding body of Gayter. The goal was wide open, another simple tap in for Bailey. Tommy looked on in awe. She was amazing! But with only one place in the team left and Tommy stuck in goal, he had no chance of making the school team. The match finished nine-two.

Mr P called everybody in. 'Well done, everybody, thank you for coming. I will put the team sheet up on the sports board tomorrow.'

Tommy was disappointed about the trial – or lack of it – but he was more concerned about finding the little shop – or big shop as it had turned out. Harry was following him but keeping a bit of a distance, sensing Tommy was in a mood. Tommy stopped, turned and waited for him to catch up.

'That free kick you guys did was pretty cool,' he said as Harry came close.

'Yeah, it was Bailey's idea, she's good, isn't she? She's bound to get in the team,' Harry replied.

Tommy nodded. 'Yeah, I know, that's the problem, I thought this was my big chance.' He sighed.

'Cheer up, Tom, you will definitely be in the team next year when the year sixes move on. Apart from Bailey, the year fives aren't all that.'

Harry had a point, to be fair to him.

'Hey, where are you going? Granville Street's this way,' Harry called.

'I'm trying to find a shop that sells old sports things. I went there the other day, it's amazing, it was near Maurice Road.'

'There are no shops near Maurice Road, Tommy, it's all houses except for the Gayters' corner shop.'

Ally Gayter's family had owned the little post office for years and, until the other day, Tommy would have been inclined to agree with Harry that there were no other shops in the area, but he knew in his bones it was there somewhere.

After about an hour of circling a half-mile radius of Maurice Road, checking each house carefully, Harry was getting increasingly annoying.

'You could search for it on the internet,' Harry suggested.

'It's not that sort of shop, Harry. It's special. You wouldn't understand,' Tommy replied. 'I know it sounds daft, but I'm sure the shop is magic!' he said, exasperated.

'It's flipping invisible, more like, come on, mate, my mum will be doing her nut in if I'm not home soon. She's only just allowed me to walk home from school on me own. She said if she can't trust me, I will have to walk to school with her again.'

Harry was right, of course, Tommy's mum would also be getting worried by now. Why couldn't they find it, though? It didn't make sense. He was getting cold in his football shorts as well. They turned the corner into Granville Street and ran flat out to the third lamppost. Tommy jumped into the air and punched the sky as he ran past the imaginary finish line.

'And the crowd goes wild, Tommy Green takes the gold for Great Britain in the one-hundred-metre sprint.'

Harry ran in a close second to take his customary silver. 'I will get that gold someday, Tommy,' he laughed, whilst trying to catch his breath.

Tommy smiled. 'I reckon you will, Haz, you're definitely getting faster.'

'See you tomorrow, mate.'

Harry walked on up to his house as Tommy pushed open

the little green gate disappointedly. Why couldn't he find the little shop? He took the key out from under the mat.

'Hello, Tommy,' said a voice behind him.

Tommy turned around to see the strange old man in his fawn-coloured overalls, small circle-rimmed glasses on the end of his nose, little grey moustache underneath.

'You dropped your reading book in my shop the other day, so I've brought it round for you. How did your trial go? Were the boots I lent you okay?' he asked.

'They were great, thanks,' Tommy lied. 'Do you want them back?'

'No, no, you keep them for the match,' said the old man. 'Right, I must really be getting back to my shop. Goodbye, Tommy.'

What match? He would never get in the team, Tommy thought to himself. He had so many questions for the strange old man.

'Mr Ree, I tried to find your shop again tonight, but it wasn't there.'

'Why were you looking for it?' he replied.

'I wanted to show Harry all the cool things you have in your shop,' Tommy replied.

'Well, that's why you couldn't find it, Tommy. But, when you really need it, it will find you.' With that, he was off down the road, whistling a tune that sounded a lot like the football round up theme. Tommy went inside.

'Dinner's ready, pet,' his mum called as he shut the door.

Tommy ate with his mum and told her how he had been stuck in goal and Harry had got a nosebleed but decided to miss out the talking cards. Maybe Harry was right, maybe he was losing it. He ran up to his room and took out the cards he'd shown Harry and looked at them closely. They were not moving, there were no wires or batteries, they were just old footie cards. Had he imagined it? He took off his football

31

socks, put the cards on top of his drawers, took out his diary and began to write.

> I hate Robin Banks. Today was even weirder than when I found Mr Ree's shop. The cards Mr Ree gave me talked; I just know it. There're some really strange things going on. The trial was a complete disaster, but the new girl Bailey was ace, maybe even better than Banksy. I won't get in, though, because Mr P put me in goal; in goal, can you believe it?! He knows nothing about football. The team sheet goes up tomorrow but I'm not sure I'll bother looking ☹ Then I came home after wasting my time looking for the little shop to find Mr Ree on my doorstep! What did he mean by 'the shop would find me'?

He finished his entry with a picture of Mr P's head on a donkey. Next, he got out his miniature football team, which consisted of two toy soldiers, a model of the Reds captain, a little yellow man from a construction kit, a dinosaur, a robot and a small plastic gorilla. This was Tommy's special team, "The Magnificent Seven", named after his dad's favourite cowboy film that they had to watch every Boxing Day. These would line up against "Robin Banks and the Mouldy Maggots". Banks was always played by a farmyard pig, Big Mac a toy doughnut, Leon Mee a plastic building brick, Ally Gayter a crocodile, Rohan De Boat a red eraser, Si Kling a pencil sharpener and Owen Cash was a toy car. He put the pencil sharpener on the bench and for the ball he used his dad's old ping-pong ball. He set all the players out in their places then realised he didn't have anyone to play Bailey – she wasn't really a gorilla or a dinosaur. *Hmm*, he thought. He went into the bathroom and looked around – shampoo, toothbrushes – then he saw it, some brand new soap, perfect.

He put the gorilla on the subs bench, which was actually an empty tissue box, alongside Si Kling, and acted out Bailey's free kick routine over and over again, only slightly differently because in this version Robin Banks ran into Leon Mee and landed on his backside and, instead of Tommy being in goal, he was in Chris Tall's position.

CHAPTER 4
Gladiator's Ready?

The next day, Tommy was standing in the main corridor, looking at the school team sheet. He couldn't resist taking a peek, although he knew full well his name wouldn't be on the list. Why would it be after his awful trial yesterday?

Liam Mackenzie
Goal Keeper (GK)

Ally Gayter   *Rohan De Boat*
Centre Back (CB)   *CB*

Wayne Dwops   *Bailey Scott*   *Owen Cash*
Right Wing (RW)   *Central Midfield*   *Left Wing (LW)*
(CM)

Leon Mee
Striker (ST)

Subs:
Ed Long
Bailey Scott
Terry Bull

Terry Bull, really? He spent most of the session doing up his laces! Bailey was only on the bench! It was obvious she was better than Wayne Dwops. Mr Point was clearly as clueless as Tommy had long suspected.

'Oi, Green, do you need a leg up so you can read the board?' Banks called down the corridor.

At least I can read it, Tommy thought.

'Hey, Mac, maybe Mr. P is considering dropping you for Green!' Big Mac pretended to look crestfallen then started sniggering.

Tommy trudged off, the laughing still ringing in his ears as he entered his classroom. Harry was already sat down, a big smile on his face.

'Hey, Haz, why are you so happy?' Tommy asked.

'Terry Bull can't play in the next match 'cause it's his nan's birthday.'

'So?' Tommy quizzed.

'So, Mr P has asked me to take his place on the bench.' Harry beamed.

Could things get any worse? Tommy felt like a building had just fallen on top of him; he was crushed completely. He should be happy for his best mate, it was great news for him, but he was filling up with jealousy, rage and grief, all at once. He felt the tears stinging his eyes but managed to croak out a, 'That's great mate,' and sat down.

'Good morning, WD4T,' chirped Mr Meener. 'Today we are going to start our DT projects. I would like you to design a sock puppet that we are going to eventually make and sell at the Christmas fair. You might want to make it with a Christmas theme, a Santa, or a reindeer, for example.'

Tommy suddenly had a vision of a large snake that had Banks's face on it and some stick-on reindeer ears for the Christmas theme. This image made him snigger, despite his pain.

'Something funny, Tommy?' Mr Meener asked.

'No, sir, sorry, sir.'

The lesson passed slowly but Tommy had decided to go with a snowman rather than his Banks-themed snake idea. The break bell sounded, and Tommy skipped out quickly. He had to go and find Bailey and persuade her to come and play for him against Banks and GO6L. He found her looking at the team sheet.

'Hey, Bailey,' Tommy called out.

The new girl turned and looked at him with a little nod.

'Hey,' she replied.

Tommy looked at the team sheet. Sure enough, Terry's name had a little line drawn through it and Hazza's name had been written next to it.

'I was just wondering if you would like to come and play football with us on the top playground?' Tommy asked.

'Yeah, that would be great. Thanks,' she said.

'You played well last night, where did you learn that free kick?' Tommy asked.

'I just make them up when I'm at home,' she replied.

Wow, could this girl be any cooler? Tommy loved to make up free kick and corner routines; he had a book full of his ideas that he would love to show her.

When they arrived at the top playground, Banks was doing keepy-uppies with Hazza's World Cup ball.

'ninety-seven, ninety-eight, ninety-nine, one hundred!'

On the hundredth kick, Banks just booted the ball in the air and Harry caught it.

'Took your time, Green. Don't mind if we borrow your mate Smith, seeing how he's in the school team now?' Banks called out. 'You don't want to play with the losers anymore, do you, Smithy?'

Harry looked sheepishly at his feet, not wanting to catch Tommy's eye.

'No problem, as long as we get Bailey,' Tommy called back.

'Ah that's nice, all the girls together,' Banks said.

The crowd started laughing.

'Then shouldn't you be on this side, Robin? I mean, anyone who spends that much time on their hair...' Bailey quipped back, smirking.

The crowd suddenly went quiet, and a familiar 'ooh'

noise reverberated around the playground.

Robin's face turned scarlet as he strolled over towards her. He was about two inches taller than Bailey and he shoved Harry's ball hard into her stomach.

Bailey didn't even flinch, instead she just calmly asked, 'Sure you don't want to join us girls then? Last chance… we could go get our nails done after school, maybe make some brownies?'

The crowd howled with laughter. Did Bailey have a death wish? Banks was absolutely fuming. He stood there, fists clenched in a sprinter position; it was obvious he was going to try and smash into Bailey first chance he got. Bailey looked at Tommy and held out her fist.

'Don't worry, we got this, Tommy, just pass me the ball from the centre.'

Tommy bumped her fist with his own and placed the ball. If he kicked the ball to Bailey, he would be sending her to the slaughter. Bailey looked straight at him steely-eyed – she clearly had a plan. He side-footed the ball perfectly to her feet. Bailey stopped it dead, expertly, with the sole of her foot and Banks flew at her just as she'd predicted. Banks launched in with a wild kick towards Bailey and the ball. Very quickly, she dragged the ball backwards so that Banks's foot swung through thin air. His momentum sent him crashing upside down onto the hard concrete floor. Then Bailey was off. Gayter was next, coming flying in using his size to intimidate her, but she just rolled the ball sideways with the sole of her foot like a matador teasing a bull. Gayter ran straight past her, landing on some of the year fives around the edge of the playground. Now Owen Cash tried to stop her. Bailey faked with a scissor move so that Cash stretched to intercept the ball. With his legs stranded in an open position, she calmly tapped the ball through them. 'Megs!' she called as she danced around him. Some of the crowd had started cheering.

A new gladiator was in town, and she was starting to win them over. Banks, now back on his feet, was bearing down on her.

'Man on!' Tommy shouted as he ran down the right wing in support.

Bailey took a quick glance over her right shoulder; Banks was almost on her. She rolled the ball backwards and balanced it on her foot. Banks tried to run right through her, but instead Bailey flicked the ball straight up into the air and span in a 360 away to her left. Banks went through the now empty space straight into the pavilion wall. As the ball came back down, Bailey simply passed it along the floor straight into Tommy's path and he gratefully smashed it inside the painted rectangle. Big Mac was standing dumbstruck, looking at the floor where his school captain lay moaning, an egg the size of a small moon on his head.

Game over.

Tommy was absolutely buzzing on the way home. He ran all the way as he was no longer talking to Harry 'The Traitor' Smith. Bailey was amazing. He kicked off his shoes and ran up to his room, grabbing his diary, and started scribbling his words down as quickly as they fell out of his head. He wrote whilst thinking aloud.

Bailey is amazing. She made Banks look like a complete donkey today and we won, we won against GO6L. Okay, Mr Meener called the game off early because Banks had a little boo boo on his head, but a win is a win. Take that, Harry Smith, and your little World Cup ball. 'Ooh I'm in the first team, so I'm dropping all my friends to be with my new first team friends.'

'You've a lot of anger in yer, lad, and that's not such a good thing for a wee man like yerself.'

Who said that? Tommy scanned the room looking for the source of the voice.

'Banks eez a bambino, though, no?'

Another voice! It was the same voices he'd heard from the cards in the medical room. Where were they? He'd left them with his socks, which were where? *Think Tommy, think.* The laundry basket. He lifted the lid slowly.

'Oh, I miei occhi!' someone cried out.

'Aye, he's right, lad, you could have warned us you were opening up, it's dark in here.' The thick Yorkshire accent again.

'Puzzolente!' And the Italian accent too.

'He's right about that too, it's also very smelly!'

Sure enough, the cards were there, lying on top of his laundry, but now both little men were quite animated, and both had hands over their eyes. Tommy rubbed his own eyes; was this a dream?

'Potami furori di qui,' said the strange little Italian winger.

'I'm not sure he speaks Italian, do you lad?' Big Alf was now looking straight at him.

'Er, no, I don't,' Tommy stammered.

'Well, what he asked you was, could you please get us out of this bin as it's a bit dark and smelly like?'

Instead, Tommy dropped the bin lid and rushed downstairs. His tea was ready, and he sat there eating it in silence, watching some soap opera on TV with his mum.

'You had a nice day, pet?' his mum asked.

'Mmm,' Tommy replied through a mouthful of sausage and chips, his mind racing. How could cards talk? It was impossible, he must be cracking up. All this nonsense with Banks and now Harry taking his place in the team, the funny little man from the shop... That was it, he was clearly going mad, there could be no other explanation.

Tommy crept back into his room to get ready for bed. He had watched three episodes of three different soaps that made literally no sense to him but strangely all had the same storyline, just with different regional accents. He flicked the footballer's belly button, and the light came on in his room. Tommy stood there listening for a minute. No talking was coming from the laundry basket anymore. He must have imagined it, but just to make sure he could sleep, he gingerly carried the basket at arm's length down to the kitchen and ran back upstairs to bed.

CHAPTER 5
Fixed Penalty

The next day, Tommy couldn't wait for the breaktime battle. It was also the big game after school and, although Tommy didn't want to watch Harry, he definitely wanted to watch Bailey. With any luck, Harry wouldn't get on and that would be the end of it because Si Kling would soon be back, and Harry would be dropped again. He hadn't said a word to Harry all morning during literacy. They'd had to pretend they were Roman settlers. Tommy made up some rubbish about looking after goats and hunting rabbits and how bad his village smelt. It was not quite Shakespeare, but twenty-three lines was a new record for Tommy. Mr Meener had been so pleased with it (especially the bit about the goats) he told him to show his work to Mr Binrite. Mr Binrite beamed and got out a shiny sticker from his drawer that said *Mr Bin Special Award* in the middle. He'd wanted them to say *Mr Binrite*, but the online shop where he had got them from limited you to just seventeen letters for free. Any extra and you had to pay more. 'I just can't justify the extra cost to the finance committee, Pam,' Tommy had heard him say once to Mrs Flett. Still, it made a change from detention.

Later, Tommy went up to the top playground, but there was no sign of Banks anywhere. The other lads from GO6L were all in a huddle. Tommy spied Chris and Artie. 'What's going on, where's Banks?'

'Haven't you heard? He has concussion. He can't play sport for four weeks!' Chris replied.

'No! Really?' Tommy was so happy; it couldn't have

happened to a nicer person. 'But what about the school match?'

'Mr P's called a lunchtime meeting for all the footballers,' Artie answered.

Just then, Bailey came over to join them. 'You heard the news about Banks?' she asked.

'Yeah, Chris just told me,' Tommy said.

'So, you going to play tonight?' Bailey asked.

'What do you mean?' quizzed Tommy.

'That's what the meeting's for, Tom, it's to see who is available to play in Banks's place,' Chris replied.

At lunchtime, the footballers all piled into Mr P's classroom. He was standing at the front, scribbling curly arrows and dotted lines all over the whiteboard in his spaghetti fashion.

'Ah, hello, boys, er and Bailey, sit down, sit down. As you know, Robin is not available for our next two matches and, with Simon out as well, we are having to bring in some extra players to fill in the gaps. We have a game tonight, as you know, against Lawton and with such short notice, I need to know by a show of hands who thinks they can stay and play tonight.'

Tommy's hand shot up. He was desperate to be picked. He glanced left and right and saw Chris, Justin Case and Philip Flop all had their hands up as well.

'Wow, okay, okay. Have you got your boots and shin pads with you?' Mr P asked.

Philip put his hand down. 'No, sir, and my mum won't be able to bring them up because she's at work.'

That left three. 'Right, well, I think the only way we can decide this fairly is a penalty shootout. Mackenzie, can you put your kit on, please?'

'Yes sir,' he replied.

Mr Point picked up his whistle from his desk and said,

'You three, kits on as well, chop, chop.'

In the pavilion, Tommy looked at the old boots that Mr Ree had given him; they looked huge. He'd waited until Chris and Justin had gone out before putting them on and, oddly, they seemed a perfect fit. He would be ridiculed, but what choice did he have? Mr P would not let him play in a school match without boots on, so he may as well try them out. Tommy walked out of the door and felt an immediate tingle in his feet. *Must be nerves*, Tommy thought. He took in the scene; the field was full of key stage two spectators. Mackenzie was in the goal, stretching, Mr P was getting balls out of a bag and Chris and Justin were talking by the penalty spot. Tommy walked towards them. His feet were still tingling. It was a cross between pins and needles and being tickled, just what he needed. Maybe the boots had spiders in them. Oh well, too late to check now!

'Nice boots, Green. Does your nan know you've borrowed them?' someone heckled from the crowd.

Tommy joined Chris and Justin. 'All right?' he asked.

Both boys just nodded, looking pensive.

'Right, Chris, you first, straight sudden death, winner gets a place on the bench for tonight's match,' Mr Point said.

Chris put one of the balls on the spot and backed away, ready to start his run up. Mr P blew his whistle and Chris ran and kicked the ball low to Big Mac's right. Mackenzie had already started to dive to his left but managed to stick out his right foot, which clipped Chris's ball. The ball went straight up in the air and over the crossbar.

'Ooh,' chorused the watching masses.

Chris looked down at the floor. Tommy felt bad for him. It was a good penalty; Mackenzie had just been lucky.

'Good try, Chris. Justin, you're next,' Mr Point said, clearly enjoying himself.

Case spotted his ball, took a single step back then looked

43

over at Mr P. The whistle blew and he took a single step passing the ball neatly into the bottom left-hand corner. Mackenzie just stood there.

'Goal!' cheered the crowd. Tommy looked over at Mackenzie and saw him wink at Case. Of course, Mac and Case were good friends. Suddenly it became clear to Tommy why Case was able to score such a soft goal. Mackenzie was going to let Case score every time so he could let his mate in the team!

'Well done, Justin. Bit too good for you, hey, Liam?' Mr Point chided. Mackenzie just nodded but Tommy saw the slight smirk on his face. 'Right, Tommy, you're next.'

Tommy selected a ball from the pile and placed it on the spot. He walked backwards, looking straight at the school number one, who looked massive in the goal. There seemed to be no space anywhere. Tommy always kicked the ball in the bottom left-hand corner whilst looking at the right-hand corner in an effort to deceive the keeper. He had spent hours down the park with Harry in goal, perfecting his run up. It was a tried and tested formula for success. His dad had said to him, 'It's all about angles, son. Imagine the penalty spot is the top of a triangle. The best players always put the ball right in the corners, giving the goalie no chance.' Tommy thought about his dad's words: angles, it's all about angles. Mackenzie stared at him, trying to make him feel even more uncomfortable – not that he needed to, his feet were buzzing like he was standing on a washing machine on full turbo spin. What was up with these boots?

'Just pass the ball into my hands, Green, so we can all go get some lunch,' Big Mac called out, making a basket with his hands.

'Not sure you need any more lunch, Mackenzie,' called out a voice from the crowd that sounded a lot like Bailey.

Some people sniggered. Mackenzie just scowled at them,

and they stopped immediately. Mr Point blew the whistle and Tommy made his familiar run towards the ball; *angles, angles*. Oh no, Mackenzie was already moving towards the bottom left-hand corner, right where Tommy wanted to kick the ball. Then the weirdest thing happened. Just as Tommy reached the ball, his feet just stopped dead in their tracks, almost making Tommy fall over. His feet were now moving on their own, his right foot chipped the ball high and straight down the middle. Mackenzie, already diving to the floor, could only watch as the ball hit the back of the practice net.

'Goal!' cheered some of the spectators, but there were also a few boos as well. Tommy looked at the ball in the net then at his feet. What had just happened? He was scared to even try and walk now.

'Good goal, Tommy, now be a good boy and move out of the way so that Justin can take his second shot. Unfortunately, Chris, you didn't make it through to round two; everyone give Chris a clap, please.'

A short ripple of applause followed Chris back to the pavilion as he walked over to get changed. Tommy shuffled slowly to one side, still looking at his feet in disbelief. Case placed another ball and took one step back. Mr P put the whistle to his lips, and then it was like déjà vu. Same one step, same corner and Mackenzie just stood there.

'Goal!' shouted the crowd, significantly louder than when Tommy had scored.

'Well, I say, Case, you could teach the England team a thing or two about penalties, couldn't you, lad?' Mr Point beamed.

How can he not see that Mackenzie is clearly cheating? Tommy thought to himself. He caught Bailey's eye in the crowd and, from the look on her face, she could also see what was going on.

'Right, Tommy, you have to score, otherwise Justin wins, okay?' Mr Point informed him.

Not that he needed reminding. *Thanks, Mr Point, for putting some more pressure on me. Mackenzie clearly knows my favourite way to kick a penalty, my feet have a mind of their own and Mackenzie is just letting Case score.* Tommy really didn't know what he was going to do. Something very strange was happening here. He'd not had any control over his feet at all when he'd scored. He placed another ball on the spot and retreated his usual seven spaces away. Lucky number seven was his dad's favourite number and now it was Tommy's. The whistle blew, snapping him out of his thoughts. He hadn't even decided where he was going to aim yet. Tommy was frozen to the spot when suddenly his feet started to move on their own again. It reminded him of the time he'd gone to a roller disco for Harry's birthday. His arms were flailing like windmill sails, it was taking all he could do to maintain his balance. Mackenzie was not moving this time. He stood stock still, arms stretched out wide, not wanting to be made to look foolish again. Tommy's right foot swung through the air but then stopped just before hitting the ball. Mackenzie dived to his right, anticipating the direction and speed of the ball, but Tommy's right foot then just tapped the ball past the keeper's exposed left.

'Goal!' came the cheer, clearly more audibly this time.

Wow, thought Tommy, *what are these boots?*

'Round three,' called out Mr P.

Justin placed his ball and took one step back. Really! Could he be any more obvious? Mackenzie was grinning, knowingly. Case stepped forward and passed the ball as before towards the same corner, but this time he misjudged his angle and the ball started to roll wide.

Mackenzie, seeing Case was about to miss, dived onto the ball and tried to throw it into the net himself, but he threw it so hard it bounced off the crossbar and safely into the crowd.

'Oh, unlucky, Justin, good effort. Right, Tommy, if you score this one, you win,' stated Mr Point proudly like he was presenting a game show.

Tommy placed his ball; his feet were tingling like crazy. The boots had got him this far, so maybe he should trust them to get him through now. He stepped back seven spaces and waited for the whistle. The whistle blew, but the strangest thing happened; his feet stopped tingling. *Oh no, what do I do now?* Tommy thought. That's when he spotted Harry in the crowd, and he knew instinctively. Tommy ran towards the ball, looking into the bottom right-hand corner and struck the ball sweetly into the opposite corner; *angles*! It worked. Mackenzie, clearly rattled, fell for the feint and dived to his left. Realising his mistake, he tried to flick out a foot the same way he saved Chris's penalty, but Tommy had hit the ball too close to the post for Mackenzie to reach it.

'Yeah!' cheered the onlookers, but Tommy wasn't sure if this was because he had scored or because everyone could now go and get some lunch!

CHAPTER 6

Pasta the Ball

All the players had got changed into the red and black kit after school. Tommy looked down at himself. The shirt was far too big. He had been given the number seven, which fit Banks perfectly, of course, but on Tommy the sleeves hung off the ends of his hands, making him look like he had noodles for arms. His shorts were so long you couldn't see his knees, but Tommy still felt six feet tall. He was so excited to be wearing the school kit he didn't care that he looked ridiculous. On top of that, he and Harry had made up and now they were standing in Mr Point's room with the other squad members. Mr P had pushed all the tables back. On the floor were red plastic pitch markers in the two-three-one formation that he wanted the team to play in and a green marker for the goalkeeper. Next to the wall were three chairs pushed together in a row.

'Right, Liam in goal,' Mr Point pointed to the floor. Big Mac sat behind the keeper position. 'Rohan and Ally defence,' Mr Point continued. The two boys followed suit and sat next to the defensive positioned markers. 'Edward, Wayne and Owen in midfield and Leon upfront, the rest of you are on the bench.' Mr P pointed to the three chairs.

Harry and Bailey sat on the first two chairs and Tommy sat on the end. Mr Point went over to the whiteboard and picked up a big red pen.

'Okay, Wayne and Owen, when you get the ball, I want you to run into these areas,' Mr P began to scribble on the board as he spoke. 'Leon, when you see them in these areas,

I want you here, Edward you then overlap into this space whilst Rohan you cover the space in here. Then Wayne, you pass the ball here whilst Owen slides in at the back post. Owen, you cut back and pass it to the edge of the box and Leon you pull the trigger!' Mr Point's voice had got higher and higher until his final pen stroke was an angry looking arrow that pointed into what looked like a goal area. 'Pass, pass, pass. Everyone got it?' the red-faced and slightly sweaty teacher asked them all.

The team all nodded in unison like they were at a rock concert. Tommy looked at Bailey and Harry, Bailey pulled a face and Harry shrugged. The board looked like an Italian restaurant had exploded.

'Leon, you're the captain in Robin's absence, go and get the CD player please, everyone else line up,' Mr Point instructed.

Mr P turned his back on them and started to rub the pasta sauce off his board as Mee pressed play on the CD player and they all filed out towards the field, Tommy at the back. His feet were not tingling now but his stomach was in knots. He had often sat on the climbing frame mocking the charade of the CD player and the farcical procession out across to the field, but now he was involved in it, he was absolutely loving every second.

Lawton were already on the pitch warming up by the far end goal. They had two good players that Ridgeway would need to be wary of. One of the defenders, Danny 'Tank' Williams, who just like his nickname suggested was incredibly strong for a year five, and their captain Jim 'Jimbo' Nasium, another year five who had played for the team last year as a year four and had finished as the league's top goal scorer with seventeen goals in just five games, two more than Banks! Mr Point blew the whistle and Jimbo shook hands with the deputising Mee. It was a Lawton centre. Both teams lined up in their opposite halves and the game was on. Tommy sat on the grass 'bench' with Bailey and Harry.

'Do you think we can win this one, Tommy?' Harry quizzed.

'Not sure, Haz, if Jimbo gets half a chance, you know he'll score. Gayter has got to stick to him like glue,' Tommy replied.

The first ten minutes were quite cagey. No one had any shots of real substance that had caused either keeper any difficulties but that was all about to change. Jimbo received the ball with his back to goal just outside the box, Gayter roared down on him. Jimbo flicked the ball backwards with the outside of his right foot past the on-rushing Gayter then quickly span to his left. Gayter went through the gap that had now opened, leaving Jimbo one-on-one with Big Mac. Jimbo collected the ball with his left foot and ran at pace towards the left-hand post. Mac, like most keepers do, came off his line and tried to narrow the shooting angle. It was too late. As soon as Jimbo saw him move, he calmly flicked the ball from his left foot onto his right and curled the ball round the keeper into the now open far post area. Mac flung himself to his left and to his credit got his fingers to the ball, but it was not enough to stop the ball nestling in the top bin.

One-nil to Lawton.

Mee kicked off but Ed Long wasn't concentrating, he was looking for his mum in the crowd, and the ball sailed past him. Jimbo was onto it like a rocket. He raced through the gap in midfield and sprinted towards De Boat. De Boat turned sideways on, trying to force Jimbo out wide like he should, but Jim Nasium was also the quickest in his school and tore past the much slower De Boat into the corner. Gayter was running across to try and keep him trapped, but this now meant there were no defenders in the box. Jimbo chipped the ball beautifully over Gayter's head towards the penalty spot.

Big Mac raced off his line to try and catch the floating ball that seemed to be just hanging in the air, but he was not quick enough. Danny 'Tank' Williams beat him to it and smashed a thunderous header into the now exposed net, whilst also knocking Big Mac into the middle of next week. Mac did not look good; he was winded following his collision. Mr P called over to the three bench warmers.

'Green, swap shirts with Mackenzie, he looks like he needs a sit down with Mrs Flett for a minute or two.'

On no, was this some sort of horrible joke? Had Mr Point not actually watched Tommy in training? Two-nil down to Lawton who were clearly playing better and now they were putting Tommy in goal. Mr P was waving the white flag. In fact, it was worse, it was like waving the white flag whilst sinking in quicksand and trying to catch a fly with chopsticks at the same time. Tommy looked at Bailey and Harry. It was clear from their faces that they agreed completely.

'Well, hurry up, boy, there's a game on, you know,' Mr Point called out impatiently.

Tommy put Big Mac's shirt straight over his own. He had now transformed from being a limp noodle into a pole-less tent. He trudged towards the goal and assumed the position just as Mee kicked off again. Long, who clearly hadn't yet spotted his mum, missed the ball and it went out for a throw-in.

'Edward, what is up with you?' Mr Point asked.

'I need the toilet, sir,' he replied, holding himself.

'Bailey, switch with Edward, and Edward, be quick about it.'

Well, that was lucky. At least with Bailey on they maybe wouldn't need to use chopsticks to catch the fly, maybe they could use a net. The Lawton winger took the throw-in, aiming for Jim Nasium. The ball arched through the air towards him. He caught it on his chest and turned De Boat easily. Looking up, he could see Tommy in the goal and, confident with the difference in size of the small boy compared to that of Mackenzie's huge frame, shot for goal. Tommy's heart froze. He tracked the ball's trajectory and knew exactly where it was heading, but was he tall enough to reach it? Surely not. Just then, his feet started to tingle and his dance on the ice started again. His feet were moving by themselves, and it took all of Tommy's concentration just to keep his balance. The ball was heading into the top left-hand corner, high to Tommy's right. Suddenly his feet did the weirdest of things. They turned Tommy around so he couldn't see the ball and so that he was now facing his own goal. A wave of panic flooded through him. Not only was he going to let in the goal, he was going to look like an idiot doing it. Then suddenly, his feet flipped him upside down and attempted a successful bicycle kick. His right foot connected sweetly with the ball sending it back up the pitch towards the halfway line. Tommy hit the ground with a bump and lay there on his back for a second, trying to comprehend what had just happened. Completely confused, he rolled onto his front just in time to see Bailey chasing the ball that was still in the air and the faces of everyone else, including Jimbo Nasium, that were full of disbelief at what they had just witnessed.

Bailey had been the first to react following this momentary lapse in concentration. She trapped the ball with the outside of her right foot and accelerated towards the Lawton goal. Leon was the second to react and chased after her in support. It was like a domino effect, players all around the pitch turning on heel in the direction of the ball, but Bailey had got the jump on them. She had just the keeper in front of her now. He was still on his goal line, making the goal a nice big target. Having Tank Williams playing in front of him, he probably didn't get called into action very often. His internal internet had clearly reconnected and now suddenly his feet and brain recognised each other again. He tried to close Bailey down, but it was too late, she had already picked her spot and calmly placed the ball past him. It looked like she had scored on her debut for certain, but Mee, who had continued his run, tapped the ball over the line from just 10cm out! A complete goal steal if ever there had been one. Instead of Bailey getting angry, she ran over to Leon to congratulate him, then she ran to the halfway line. *Total class*, Tommy thought, still lying on his front. Suddenly, his sightline was obscured by a pair of black socks and a hand that was leaning down towards him. Gayter looked down at him.

'Wow, Tommy, how did you do that?' he asked.

The honest answer was he had no idea, other than he thought he had magic boots on, but as that would just sound crazy, he went with a simple, 'Dunno,' and accepted the hand up.

The dramatic events that had led to the Ridgeway goal seemed to have taken the wind out of the sails of the Lawton team and at halftime it remained two-one.

The players got their drinks bottles and huddled around Mr Point, who was now hurriedly moving magnetic counters around his mini tactics board. Harry came to stand near Tommy and patted him on the back.

'I thought you said you were rubbish in goal, mate?' A big smile took up most of the space on his face. Tommy just shrugged, still dumbfounded as he tried to tune into Mr Point's master plan of attack.

The two teams lined back up, only now Big Mac was in goal again and Harry was on for De Boat, who had been struggling to cope with Jimbo's pace. Tommy sat by Ed Long, who had now returned from the toilet but had missed the goal and the halftime team talk. It was with relief but also some disappointment that he now sat there watching again.

Ridgeway kicked off with Mee passing to Owen Cash. Cash was more alert, at least, and Ridgeway managed to keep the ball for longer than thirty seconds. Jimbo went close a couple of times, hitting the post and the bar, but was getting fewer chances with Bailey now dominating in midfield – although the only Ridgeway players passing to her were Harry and Wayne! Bailey was managing to intercept most of the Lawton passes getting through to Jimbo and Harry was stuck to him like glue, giving him less time and space when he did get the ball. At the other end, Tank was keeping Leon and Owen Cash quiet, reducing them to shooting from long range. The clock ticked on, and it was looking more and more likely Lawton were going to take all three points.

With just five minutes to go until full time, Ridgeway won a corner. Owen Cash went over to take it, as usual, but Bailey was already by the flag holding the ball.

'Give it here, I take the corners and you're just a girl,' he snarled.

'Ah, thanks for noticing,' Bailey quipped.

She dropped the ball to the floor, trapping it expertly. As Cash approached, she flicked the ball out towards him with her right foot. The ball hit him on his knee and ricocheted to his left-hand side. Bailey was already moving and was back on the ball before anyone else on the pitch had reacted; some of the Lawton players were walking towards the goal and not even facing the right way.

'Watch out!' shouted Nasium, who was now sprinting to close her down from the halfway line.

Tank turned around and rushed to block her from shooting. Bailey shaped up to shoot but Tank was blocking her path and getting closer, so instead she passed to Leon Mee, who was near the penalty spot. He wasn't expecting the pass but stopped the ball with his left foot then hurriedly tried to make a shooting angle. Bailey ran past the oncoming Tank and on towards Leon, getting to him just as he was about to shoot and dragging the ball backwards, causing Leon to air kick and fall flat on his backside. Nasium was right behind her now, running at full speed. Tank was closing in on her left – she was going to get clattered by them both. Bailey was facing the goal but then she did the strangest thing. Instead of shooting, she back-heeled the ball out of the box at the last minute and allowed both boys to run into her. Bailey went down heavily underneath them both, as all three collided and landed on top of Leon Mee, who let out a muffled, 'Ow, geroff!'

'Penalty!' cried out Mr Point.

Nasium and Williams looked crestfallen, realising they had just been duped. Leon Mee unfolded himself from the floor and went to get the ball.

'Sir,' Bailey called out. 'Do you think Tommy should take the penalty? He was amazing at lunchtime, wasn't he?'

Mr Point looked up to one side as some people do when they are engrossed in thought.

'Yes, Bailey, great idea,' he replied after a couple of seconds. 'Green, swap with Cash quickly.'

Tommy was petrified; what was Bailey playing at? This goal could tie the game and give Ridgeway a vital point. Cash was walking towards him with a look of pure disgust on his face. Tommy looked at the floor and made his way towards the penalty spot gingerly. Leon Mee was protesting with Mr Point as he approached them.

'But sir, I'm the captain and he's only in year four!'

'I've made my decision, Leon, now give me the ball,' Mr P demanded.

Mee looked daggers at Tommy.

'You'd better not miss, Green,' he snarled.

Mr Point passed Tommy the ball and he placed it on the bright white spot. He looked up to see what the Lawton keeper was doing but he was not there, the goal was empty. He turned and looked at Mr P quizzically, who just pointed towards the goal. Tommy turned back to look just as Tank Williams marched towards the goal, now squeezed into the keeper's jersey. Oh no, Tank looked absolutely huge in the goal, maybe even bigger than Mac. Tommy gulped.

Bailey appeared at his shoulder. 'You've got this, Tommy Green. Now show them what you can do.' She bumped his fist and Tommy smiled weakly. He stepped slowly backwards until he was at his much-practised familiar seven paces. He looked at the red and black custom nets; was this really happening? He had dreamt of this moment for so long. The silence was so loud in Tommy's ears it was deafening. Why were his boots not tingling? Now was the time he needed them most, surely. Not a murmur, not even an irritating itch was coming from his feet. He had no choice; he was on his own for this one. The whistle blew. Tommy made his run looking into the bottom right-hand corner and then he passed the ball in the bottom left. Tank fell for the feint and dived the wrong way.

'Goooaaalll!' shouted the assembled Ridgeway supporters. Harry and Bailey were the first to get to Tommy, wrapping their arms around him and jumping up and down.

'Get in, Tommy, you've just scored for school, mate!' Harry beamed at him.

Two-two.

The smile on Tommy's face was actually hurting him but he felt ten feet tall. He slowly turned around on the spot, absorbing the scenes of hysteria unfolding in front of him. He wanted to savour this moment for as long as he could.

After the match, Harry and Tommy raced home, Tommy narrowly edging the victory. He waved goodbye to Harry and went up to his room. He took his boots out and looked at them carefully. Banks was right, they looked ridiculous, but there was obviously something very special about them.

56

'Lo sono bagnato,' said a small voice.

'I'm wet too, lad, and I'm not due a bath until December!' said another.

Tommy had completely forgotten about the cards in all the excitement. He looked over at his bedside drawers where the sound had come from. He slowly opened the top drawer and saw a note his mum had written.

Pet, these have been through the washing machine, but I have dried them out on the radiator, and they look okay. They're quite old, mind, were they your dad's? They might be worth a bit of money if you took them to the museum or something. Mum x

Tommy took the cards out of the drawer and looked at them carefully. They were a bit damp still. Both men looked like they had been in the rain but were now staring wide-eyed at his boots.

'Stupefacente,' said a small voice.

'Aye, Toni, amazing is right. Do you know who those boots used to belong to, lad?' Alf asked.

'No,' Tommy replied.

'The great Stanley Martin, that's who.'

'Who was Stanley Martin?' Tommy asked, a little frightened and unsure if he was seeing and hearing things again.

'Mamma Mia!' said the little Italian man, putting his hand on his head.

'Stan 'The Man' Martin played for England back in the day. Clever little winger, scored over 400 career goals and those there were his boots, lad.'

Tommy turned the boots over in his hand slowly; over 400 goals, wow indeed! He now looked at both of the funny little men in more detail.

'How come you can talk?' Tommy asked.

'Perché non sono un bambino,' the little Italian man said.

'What did he say?' Tommy asked.

'He said because he is not a baby,' the Yorkshire man said. 'Toni, talk to him in English.'

'Mi Ingleesh iz nut gud,' Toni replied.

'Ay but better than his Italian any road,' Alf chuckled.

'Okay, okay, si hai ragiore,' Toni looked straight at Harry. 'Wee 'ere to 'elp yoo bee grate mayor.'

'He means great player, lad,' Alf translated. 'We were asked to help you, so if you want any advice, like, you just have to ask us.'

'But why me? How is any of this possible?'

'Magia,' Toni exclaimed.

'Aye, Toni, magic,' Alf said. 'To be honest, lad, we're not altogether sure how it works ourselves. One minute we're up there playing the longest game of football of our lives with some of the greatest players the world has ever seen, and then we're down here talking to you. Please don't be scared, though, we mean you no harm.'

'Onion less, heeza putz me in da smeelee been again,' Toni retorted, flicking his hair.

'Aye, lad, we could do without that, if you don't mind,' Alf laughed.

Tommy smiled and promised he would not put them in the laundry basket or the washing machine again. He grabbed his diary and began to write.

I scored for school today. Unbelievable, I know! It was just a penalty but, as dad used to say, they all count. Have that, Banks!

He finished his entry by drawing a picture of the penalty and Bailey and Harry celebrating with him. He put Stan's boots under his pillow and placed the strange football cards carefully in his top drawer, saying goodnight to both of them, which felt a bit surreal.

'Tea's ready, pet.'

Tommy raced downstairs to tell his mum all about the game, still not quite ready to discuss magic boots and talking cards yet!

The next day, everyone at school was buzzing. People were talking in groups and pointing over at Tommy. Harry gave his mate a nudge. 'Ah, you're proper famous now, Tommy. I heard Banks was spitting feathers when he heard you'd scored, and only being a year four an' all.'

Tommy smiled. That was the icing on the cake right there. Bailey saw the two boys and came over. 'Hey, you two, great game last night, wasn't it?' she asked.

'Yeah, you were brilliant, Bailey,' Tommy replied.

'So were you. What about that save you made? I've never seen anything like it! Everyone is talking about it today. That girl Emma in year five was saying to some other girls in the toilets, "He lives next door to me; I've known him for years." You have a proper fan there, Tommy,' Bailey teased.

Tommy blushed. Emma was talking about him. Why? She had never even spoken to him before. The last few weeks may have been weird, but Tommy was not complaining, he was on clouds nine, ten and eleven!

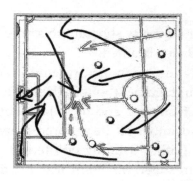

CHAPTER 7

Oh When the Saints

Tommy had been waiting all week for the team sheet to go up for the next game. It was an away game the following night after school. He ran down the corridor and found Bailey already studying the sheet.

Liam Mackenzie
GK

Ally Gayter   Rohan De Boat
CB   CB

Wayne Dwops   Bailey Scott   Owen Cash
RW   CM   LW

Leon Mee
ST

Subs:
Edward Long
Harry Smith
Tommy Green

'No need for a penalty shootout this time, Tommy, you're on the bench,' Bailey beamed.

'Yeah, and you're in centre mid,' Tommy replied. 'Gonna be a tough game, though, they're top of the league with two wins from two and have Jack Pott in their team. He's really good, and look, he's scored seven goals already, one more than Jimbo.' Tommy pointed to a piece of paper next to the team sheet. Mr Point was the fixture secretary for all the schools in the league, so he'd printed out the league table and top goal scorers list for all the school to see.

League Table

	W	D	L	Pts	F	A	GD
All Saints	2	0	0	6	12	5	+7
Ridgeway	1	1	0	4	9	4	+5
Thornside	1	0	1	3	6	9	-3
Lawton	0	2	0	2	7	7	0
Old Green	0	1	1	1	8	11	-3
Hawksmoor	0	0	2	0	4	10	-6

Key: W = *Wins* D = *Draws* L = *Losses* Pts = *Points* F = *Goals For* A = *Goals Against* GD = *Goal Difference*

Top Goal Scorers

Jack Pott (All Saints) 7
Jaun Tu (Old Green) 7
Jim Nasium (Lawton) 6
Robin Banks (Ridgeway) 4
Leon Mee (Ridgeway) 3
David Jones (All Saints) 3
Markus Absent (Thornside) 3
Mike Raphone (Thornside) 2
Riley Thompson (Hawksmoor) 2
Ronny Thompson (Hawksmoor) 2
Ray Deo (All Saints) 2

Daniel Williams (Lawton) 1
Owen Cash (Ridgeway) 1
Thomas Green (Ridgeway) 1
Robert Smyth (Thornside) 1

Some people frowned on having the league displayed, but Tommy loved it. Working out goal difference was one of the only maths activities Tommy enjoyed. He was all about football statistics and could tell you who all the best players in the town were. He had played with many of them in the summer holidays down the park. Sometimes it could be twenty a side! All the local boys would congregate in the park and play across from one set of trees to the other. When it was really hot the cricket club would put the sprinklers on so at halftime the lads would race through the water as quickly as they could. The object was not to get wet but soon they would all be dancing in the spray to cool down. It reminded Tommy of international football. It didn't matter what school you played for when you were picked for a side in the park, school loyalties were dropped, and you were all teammates for the next three or four hours or until the lad with the ball had to go home for his tea!

'Who is Jaun Tu?' Bailey asked.

'He moved here this year from Portugal. My mate Neil who plays in goal for Thornside knows one of the lads from Old Green and he says he was on the books for one of the top Portuguese sides before his family moved here. He reckons he has crazy skills and is better than Banksy, not that Banksy would ever admit it. We're just lucky that the rest of Old Green are not up to much,' Tommy replied.

'Well, there is no "I" in team but there is a "me",' Bailey said with a cheeky wink and, with that, she went back to her classroom.

Harry and Tommy made their way home, but instead of racing each other, they were now walking slowly with Emma Nently and some of her friends. Emma was holding Tommy's hand and Harry was trudging behind them with his ball, sniggering to himself. Tommy just kept scowling over his shoulder whilst trying to stop his hands from sweating.

Emma had asked him at the school gate if he would walk her home and Tommy had just nodded, suddenly unable to make his mouth work. She had insisted on holding his hand but had ignored him the whole time they were walking, telling her friends instead how she had told them all she knew him, and Tommy was now her boyfriend. This had made Harry snort snot out of his nose, which landed on the back of Emma's skirt. Fortunately, only Tommy had noticed. When they got to Tommy's house Emma made a big theatrical gesture of leaning down and kissing Tommy on the cheek and saying goodbye to all her friends who were giggling. Tommy felt very hot and fumbled for the key under the mat, trying to get inside as quickly as possible. Harry continued up the road, whistling the wedding march tune, still sniggering to himself.

'Night, Tommy!' Emma called out, blowing him a kiss across the small dividing hedge.

Tommy instinctively ducked the imaginary kiss and fell backwards into a bush. He looked up to reply but Emma had already gone inside. He hoped that she hadn't seen him fall over.

That night, Tommy got out his assortment of fantasy footballers and practised his corner number one routine. The Reds' own Captain Marvel took all the corners, mainly because he was the only one who had poseable arms but also because it was the character that was always chosen to portray Tommy. The signal to the ragtag team was one arm up that told the player on the near post to run towards the corner flag. The player on the post was Bailey, now a slightly damp bar of soap. His mum had wanted it back for her bath, but Tommy didn't mind because it smelt nicer out of its wrapper. Tommy played the ping-pong ball along the floor to Bailey and then started a run towards the area. Bailey passed the ball back at exactly forty-five degrees so that Tommy could whack it in the far top bin.

'Goal!'

'Il gol!' came a joint cheer from his dad's old wallet. Tommy had made a makeshift stand for Alf and Toni to watch the game from. He had opened the wallet into a V-shape and slid the cards into the space for credit cards endways up so they could see all the action.

'That is a good corner routine, lad, did you make it up yourself?' Alf asked.

'Yeah, I've made up loads and write them down in this book,' Tommy replied as he pulled out a small black leather book from the same place he kept his diary. It was just an old address book his mum had given him to use as scrap paper, but over the gold-embossed word "addresses", Tommy had glued a piece of paper that simply said, "Top Secret". It held over thirty different corner, free kick and throw-in routines that Tommy had invented over hours of playing with his toys in his bedroom. One day, when he was old enough, he would coach the best team in the world and showcase his ideas on his way to winning the World Cup.

'Show us another one then, lad,' Alf requested.

Tommy set up for corner number two. This time, Tommy positioned Harry, who was being played by the dinosaur because it was orange like his hair, by the halfway line. Bailey was back on the near post, the two soldiers and the robot were on the edge of the area. Tommy stuck both his character's arms in the air to signal he was taking corner number two. Bailey made a run to the corner to fake a short one and to draw Owen Cash – the racing car – off the near post. Harry began his run from the halfway line near to where the corner was being taken and angled his run in an arc towards the area. Tommy passed the ball in front of him perfectly and Harry smashed that into the top bin as well.

'Ger-in there!' Alf called out.

'Magnifico!' Toni agreed.

Tommy loved his new friends being involved in his imaginary games; it was nice to just have someone to talk to about his ideas. He missed his dad.

The next day finally came. Tommy had kept his head down and worked hard, not wanting to give any teachers the chance to keep him in. Also, he was avoiding Emma Nently, who had started sending him pictures of the two of them getting married with soppy love hearts drawn all over the place. He'd thought he liked Emma because she was pretty but, to be honest, he did not like all the slushy stuff that came with having a girlfriend. Girlfriend? He still hadn't said more than yes, thank you and hello to her! At break and lunch, he had stayed in the library reading about Stanley Martin so that he could save all his energy for the match. Stanley Martin had played at the same club all his career and won the league three times. Nicknamed 'Stan the Man' by his adoring fans, he was famous for his tricks and flicks and acrobatic goals. Tommy felt for his boots in his bag. Oh no! He'd left them at home in the kitchen. Tommy felt sick. Mr P never let people play without their proper kit on match days. 'Fail to prepare, then prepare to fail,' he always said. What was he going to do? He ran to find Harry and Bailey and tell them. They were both talking by the drink fountain, but Emma and her friends were blocking the corridor. Tommy grabbed a woolly hat and a scarf out of the lost property box and pulled the hat right down over his ears whilst wrapping the scarf around his nose and mouth. He then put his head down and walked quickly past the group of girls.

'When we get married, we will have a big house and seven children and a dog and two cats…' Even with the hat over his ears, Tommy could hear Emma boasting to her friends.

He reached Harry and Bailey in his makeshift disguise.

'Hey, Tommy, why are you dressed like you're going skiing?' Bailey asked.

'I'm trying to avoid Emma and her friends; she's driving me batty. If this is what marriage is like, I'm going to live on my own with just the dog and two cats,' Tommy replied. Harry pulled a quizzical face. 'Don't ask,' Tommy cut him off before he could speak. 'More importantly, I left my boots at home and Mum is at work, so I can't play tonight.'

'I have a spare pair with me, Tommy,' Harry said. 'They might be a bit big, but better than nothing.'

What else could Tommy do? He would not have time to go home. After school, the three of them got changed in the pavilion and Harry's dad had given Tommy and Bailey a lift to the game because both of their parents were at work. Mr Point had given them all a letter saying they needed to meet at All Saints school at 3.45pm for a 4pm kick off. With it getting closer to the end of the year, it was getting dark early, and this would be the last game before the Christmas break.

Tommy had Harry's spare boots on. They were like flippers on his small feet, they didn't feel right at all. With any luck, Tommy wouldn't get on and he could just watch Bailey play. The All Saints players were warming up in their black-and-white striped kit. Jack Pott, clearly identifiable because he was the biggest player in their team, was wearing the captain's armband and leading the warm-up whilst their teacher was talking to Mr Point. The rest of the Ridgeway team were over by the side putting their bags and drinks bottles in a pile. Mr Point ran over to the group, tracksuit on, whistle and stopwatch around his neck.

'Right, boys – and, er, Bailey, of course – you know where you're all playing. Leon is captain, let the ball do the work, pass and move, be ready before them, keep it simple, pull the trigger when you can and win your individual battles,' he recited.

Mr Point put his hand into the middle of the huddle and the others placed their hands on top, all except Tommy. By the time he had realised what was going on, he couldn't reach the top of the hand pyramid, so settled with putting his hand on Harry's arm.

'One, two, three, Ridgeway!' they all chorused.

Tommy sat with Harry on the grass by the side of the pitch trying to work out Mr Point's team talk. Keep what simple? Let the ball do the work? What were the team meant to do then, stand and watch? The whistle blew. It was a Ridgeway centre. Mee played the ball back towards Gayter, who thumped it down the pitch. Owen Cash was running down the left wing expecting the long ball. He controlled the ball on his chest with his back to goal. Davey Jones, one of the All Saints defenders, closed him down quickly. Cash saw him out of the corner of his eye and feinted to turn inside but, at exactly the right second, span in the opposite direction, taking the ball out wider instead. He only had the goalkeeper and empty space in front of him, so accelerated towards the goal. Bailey was running parallel with him through the middle of the pitch, Jack Pott hot on her heels. The Saints keeper came off his line just enough for Cash to try and chip him. The ball sailed over the keeper but hit the crossbar and ricocheted back towards Bailey. Bailey controlled the ball on her thigh and was just swinging her leg to volley the ball into the waiting net when Jack Pott barged her off balance and turned away with the ball. It was a clear foul, but the All Saints teacher did not look at all interested. Mr Point was jumping up and down like his feet were on fire, shouting, 'Referee! Referee!' but to no avail.

I knew it was going to be tough, Tommy thought. Jack Pott had run into the Ridgeway half and played a pass out wide to their right winger Dan Druff. Dan Druff was a big lad, standing head and shoulders above the rest, but De Boat tackled him easily and played the ball back to Cash, but this time Davey Jones was ready for him and also won the ball back quickly.

'Well done, Davey, keep him in your locker,' one of the parents shouted. Tommy guessed it was Davey's dad.

The game followed a similar pattern of turnovers with some bruising tackles that only seemed to be fouls when it was Ridgeway doing the tackling. There was only a minute to go until halftime when Bailey tackled Jack Pott just outside of the Ridgeway area. It was a good tackle, she turned and started to run towards the Saints' half when the whistle blew.

'Free kick,' said the referee.

What? No way! Tommy thought. Mr Point's feet immediately set on fire again, this time accompanied with him booting one of the spare balls into a tree. Over the other side of the pitch, some of the parents were getting into a heated debate over the free kick decision. It was mainly the dads, but Leon Mee's mum was waving her umbrella at one man who was now hiding behind his wife. Jack Pott picked up the ball and placed it just outside the area. In the Ridgeway wall, Leon, Owen and Wayne stood looking nervously at the length of the run-up that captain Jack had retreated to. The whistle blew and Pott charged towards the ball, the Ridgeway wall jumped in every direction to avoid being hit as Jack smashed the ball through the now open space straight into Big Mac's stomach. The big keeper keeled over and spilt the ball straight into the path of Davey Jones, who calmly passed it into the vacant net.

Halftime: One-nil.

The team all huddled around Mr Point when Tommy spotted movement out of the corner of his eye. Oh no, Emma was marching towards him.

'Tommy Green, I cannot go out with a substitute, you are making me look silly,' she squawked. 'Robin has asked me out and if you do not get on and score a goal then I will have no choice but to dump you!'

With that, she turned on her heel and marched back over to the spectators. Mr Point scribbled furiously over the small whiteboard he'd brought with him whilst moving little red magnetic counters into different positions. It seemed strange to Tommy that Owen Cash was not a car. A lot of what Mr Point was saying didn't make sense to him and, judging by the faces in the little huddle, it was clear the rest of the team were equally dumbfounded. The worst decision he made was subbing Bailey with Ed Long. Jack would be licking his chops at the prospect of playing against Long. Ed was so skinny that, if the wind got up, he'd struggle to stay anchored to the pitch, but at least he might be able to get the ball down from the tree. Tommy smiled to himself; every cloud, heh!

The game restarted and it was panning out exactly how Tommy had predicted. Jack Pott was now playing with more freedom because Ed Long was rushing into tackles without looking. He terrorised Gayter and De Boat, he was winning all the duels and scored his first goal within five minutes of the restart. Two-nil Saints. Robin Banks had been over the other side of the pitch with his dad but now both of them were striding towards Mr Point. Tommy could not quite hear what was being said but he caught the odd word. Something about sponsorship being taken back, associated with winners not losers, pulling fingers out? Then they both stormed back around to the other side. Mr Point was looking pensive as Ridgeway continued to squander possession.

Tommy picked up Mr Point's magnetic tactics board and started showing Bailey and Harry some of his corner routines. He was just explaining number three when a cheer went up over the other side and Jack Pott was marching back to the centre circle with the ball under his arm. He'd just scored his second goal. When he got to the middle of the pitch, he just stood there with the ball now under his foot, arms folded, and the All Saints team standing around the circle saluting him. The Ridgeway boys looked dejected.

Mr Point clearly panicked, shouted, 'Sub!' and then called Tommy, Harry and Bailey over. 'Right, you three, last throw of the dice,' he said to them.

'Dice, sir?' Tommy questioned.

'Look, just get on the pitch and score me some goals, will you? We're embarrassing ourselves out there,' he said exasperatedly.

Ed, Wayne and Rohan made way for 'The Three Amigos' as Bailey had called them whilst they had been sitting on the bench. Harry in defence, Bailey in the middle and Tommy on the right. Harry's boots still felt very loose, even though Tommy had put half a roll of loo paper in each boot.

'Oh no,' shouted a familiar voice. 'We've just thrown in the towel!' Robin Banks stood there laughing with his dad.

Tommy looked away quickly as Banks caught his eye. It was a Ridgeway centre. Twelve minutes to go, three-nil down. Not good. Leon kicked the ball to Owen Cash, who played it back to Gayter, ready for the big hoof upfront. Pott was already retreating, expecting the long ball, but instead of thumping it, Ally just passed the ball to Bailey.

'Go on, Bailey, get us a goal,' he shouted at her.

Most of the players were all sitting on the edge of the All Saints box expecting the ball to have been played there. This meant there was a lot of open grass between them and Bailey. She knocked the ball out of her feet and accelerated quickly down the middle of the pitch into the All Saints' half. Pott reacted quickest and ran to close her down, followed by the other Saints players. Cash and Mee just stayed upfront, shaking their heads at Gayter like he'd betrayed them. Bailey spotted the opportunity and just scooped the ball high over the charging army in front of her. The ball landed perfectly at Owen's feet, and he turned and ran at the All Saints goal. With no offside, Mee and Cash were now two on one with the keeper. The Saints players tried to turn and close them down, but it was too late, they'd been duped. Cash drew the keeper towards him and then just passed the ball square for Leon to tap into the empty net. Three-one, eleven minutes to go. Not good, but definitely better.

All Saints kicked off. Tommy anticipated Jack's pass to the Saints left winger, Miles Aypart. Tommy had seen him creeping into the Ridgeway half before the centre was taken, intercepted the ball and tried to run into the Saints half, but with the large boots on he was struggling to reach his usual speed. Pott closed in on him like a lion hunting a wounded gazelle.

'Tommy!' Bailey shouted. She'd made a diagonal run in between Pott and Jones and was calling for a pass. Tommy kicked the ball unceremoniously towards her. It was not the best pass, but it made it. Bailey ran with the ball at Davey Jones, just as Pott smashed into Tommy. He hit him so hard that his left boot flew off into the air, followed by two or three streamers of toilet roll. Lying on his back, Tommy watched upside down as Bailey rainbow-flicked the ball over the open-mouthed Jones and bore down on the Saints goal. Pott was still getting up off the floor and watched helplessly as Bailey delicately chipped over the Saints keeper into the net. What a great way to score your first goal for school. Bailey ran over to Tommy and hauled him up, just as Harry and Ally Gayter arrived to help celebrate.

'Great pass, Tommy!' She beamed.

'Great goal!' Tommy smiled back as he got to his feet.

Three-two with just under ten minutes to go. Not too bad. Ridgeway had a chance to get something out of the game now.

Saints kicked off again, but this time played the ball back into their own half for safety. Jack Pott was sitting much deeper now, helping the Saints defend their slender lead. Ridgeway had the momentum, though. Tommy – having retrieved and re-stuffed Harry's left boot – was slowly adjusting to his larger feet and playing a bit more like his old self. Harry was playing well alongside Gayter, although they were having a lot less to do with Jack sitting so far back. The odd long shot he did have Mac had picked out of the air quite comfortably. Tommy collected the ball wide on the right following a pass from Bailey and ran towards Davey Jones. The much larger boy stretched for the ball as Tommy hugged the sideline. With Davey's body weight committed in one direction, Tommy easily cut inside him with a deft flick of his right foot and Jones slid off the pitch into Leon Mee's mum, who then fell backwards and whacked Robin Banks on the head with her umbrella as she went down. Tommy didn't have time to look, but the sound of Robin Banks in clear pain gave him a deeply satisfied feeling. Leon Mee was running into the box on the back post. Pott, who was on the edge of the area, was blocking a pass along the floor, so Tommy crossed the ball in the air around the inside of him. The ball landed perfectly in front of Leon, who shot low towards the goal. The Saints keeper got a foot to it and directed it around the post for a corner. After Bailey's corner against Lawton, Mr P had given her the corner-taking responsibility, which had clearly infuriated Owen Cash. Bailey collected the ball and told Tommy to stand on the front post. She put one hand in the air and Tommy ran towards her. They played a quick one-two and Bailey hit the ball hard towards the far top bin. The Saints players were slow to react, and the ball hit the crossbar and bounced down over the line. Tommy ran to Bailey to celebrate as Jack Pott kicked the ball into the crowd.

'Throw-in,' The referee called.

'What do you mean throw-in?!' shouted Mr Point.

'The ball did not cross the line,' The referee retorted. 'Throw-in to Ridgeway.'

No way! Tommy was furious, it was clearly a goal, and the Saints players had all put their heads down because they'd known it was a goal as well. The parents were kicking off again. Leon's mum was back on her feet waving her brolly around. Robin Banks's dad was calling at Mr Point to do something and Robin Banks was sitting on the floor with his hand on his head in between two mums who were turning the air blue. There were only a few seconds left of the game and a draw away at All Saints would have been an okay result, but a loss would mean All Saints would be five points clear of Ridgeway and top of the table. Bailey took the throw-in quickly to Leon. He turned and ran past Jack Pott, who was trying to trap him in the corner.

'Leon!' Bailey called.

Mee, with nowhere to go, back-heeled the ball to Bailey, who hit a shot at goal. The ball smacked the bottom of the post and ricocheted straight back to Tommy. The keeper was on the floor after diving to try and stop Bailey's shot – empty net, easy goal. Tommy thumped the ball goalwards, only for Harry's boot to fly off in the process, so that the ball just trickled towards the goal and the boot flew into the net instead. The Saints keeper just picked the ball up and kicked it clear.

Full time: Three-two to Saints.

'Nice one, Green,' Cash hissed as he went past.

Tommy was desperately trying to put Harry's boot back on and hoping the ground would open up and swallow him. Harry came over and helped him up.

'Unlucky, Tommy,' he said as he hauled Tommy back to his feet.

Tommy was utterly distraught. He'd had the chance to

equalise the game but now had made himself look ridiculous.

Robin Banks came over towards them. 'What a joke,' he gloated. 'Thank goodness Si and I will be back after Christmas so that you two won't have to embarrass the school anymore.'

'Well, at least they don't run into brick walls with their heads,' Bailey announced as she came over. 'I saw on the telly that they're still doing two-for-one at the opticians if you hurry.'

Harry and Tommy tried not to smirk, but it was impossible – both boys guffawed out loud as Banks stormed off.

'Well, at least we know your corner works, Tommy,' Bailey said.

The Three Amigos trudged off to find Harry's dad, who was trying to stop Leon Mee's mum taking off the referee's head with her umbrella!

CHAPTER 8

Feeling a little sheepish

With all inter-school sport now suspended until the spring, and with the weather turning bad, it brought with it the joy of wet playtimes. Tommy hadn't kicked a ball for weeks. The sports noticeboard showed that All Saints were still top of the league, Thornside second, and Ridgeway had dropped to fourth. The day after the Saints game had been unbearable. Robin Banks had goaded Tommy every chance he could get for missing the open goal. Emma had also dumped him, although he was secretly a little relieved about that. Tommy had not realised how much attention girlfriends needed. Emma was also quite tall, so when they walked around school holding hands it looked like he was walking with his mum. Something Banks had been quick to point out on several occasions! At least he still had Harry and Bailey, whom he'd spent most of his breaktimes with, creating cool free kick and corner routines.

Tommy was sitting in the main hall dressed as what was allegedly a sheep. The costume was so old and battered it made him look more like a white-haired caveman, as if he needed any more humiliation. Harry was all right, he was dressed as a king, Bailey was a shepherd and, of course, Robin Banks, as head boy, was Joseph. Tommy was sure that Banks would have preferred to have been God, but thank goodness that part was taken by Mr Meener, who kept putting on a deep voice when he read the Bible over the microphone. Tommy was bored. His part basically saw him walk on, which took all of six seconds, and then sit crossed-legged with arms folded for half an hour next to a plastic doll covered in straw. It really smelt too. Mr Meener was supposed to have picked up some fresh straw on his way home from school but had forgotten and so had taken some out of the school rabbit hutch. Tommy was desperate to let out the occasional baa to make it more obvious he was a sheep, but had been on strict instructions to sit still or else he would miss the Christmas party. His mum had said she was coming to watch the play and would try to video it. Tommy couldn't think of anything worse. It was all very well having to suffer the humiliation this year, but to be reminded of it over and over, every time someone visited! Tommy had been trying to sit next to Amber Dextrous from year three for the last four days because she'd just returned to school after having chicken pox and he thought, if he could inhale her germs, he would be too ill to be in the nativity, but Amber had now become convinced Tommy fancied her and kept giggling and waving at him with both hands whenever she saw him.

After rehearsals, Tommy went to find Harry and Bailey in the library. They were sitting at a small table with a collection of objects from both of their pencil cases.

'Hey, Tommy!' Bailey called out. 'Just in time, we need a goalie, have you got your rubber?'

Tommy rifled through his bag, found his pencil case, then emptied it out onto the table. He'd forgotten that his two football cards were in there as well and they flopped out onto the table with an assortment of felt tip pens, pencils, a ruler and half an eraser.

'Woh! What are these cards, Tommy?' Bailey asked, turning the nearest one over. She looked at Alf's card carefully. 'Looks like a defender.' Bailey swapped Alf with a yellow pencil sharpener on the table. 'This one can be Harry,' she said. Bailey was now looking at Toni's card. 'These must be over fifty years old.'

'They were my dad's, my mum found them in the loft,' Tommy lied.

'Cool, can I be this one?' Bailey asked as she picked up a glue stick and replaced it with Toni.

'Yeah, all right, as long as I can be the pineapple rubber,' Tommy laughed nervously, secretly relieved that the cards did not seem to be moving.

The three friends set up a wall by standing four thick felt tip pens up on their ends and using two of their water bottles as goalposts. Bailey put Toni in front of the rainbow wall facing to the right and used a 5p coin for the ball.

'Right, I call this free kick "Fetch",' Bailey said as she quickly positioned an assortment of other objects.

Tommy had a pad out and started drawing the positions so that he could add it to his playbook later.

'You know when people play fetch with their dog,' Bailey started to explain as she placed the pineapple rubber on the left-hand side of the wall. 'Sometimes the owner pretends to throw the stick and the dog tears after it, but it's really still in the owner's hand and the dog is looking all confused? This free kick is based on that.' Bailey put Alf's card next to the pineapple and a ruler next to Toni. 'Okay, watch this,' she said. She made the pineapple eraser run in front of the wall and then sharply turn towards goal, then she made Toni's card step over the 5p football. 'As soon as Tommy runs in front of the wall, I pretend to kick it to him. The wall will be confused and move slightly to their left following Tommy to where they think the ball is going. I step over the ball as if I am going to kick it but completely miss it and run after Tommy.' Bailey moved the pens from the wall slightly, so they looked like they were chasing Tommy and then pointed to Alf's card. 'Look, Harry now has more space,' she continued. She made the ruler move towards the 5p and pretended to make it kick it towards

Alf's card. 'Tommy's run should have confused the keeper as well, so Harry may be able to shoot first time. Tommy, you would follow the shot in case there is a rebound,' Bailey explained.

Tommy was scribbling all this down on his pad as quickly as he could, concentration etched on his face.

'What do you think?' Bailey asked.

'I like it,' Harry replied. 'Can you imagine if we did this on the playground against Banksy, Tommy?'

Tommy looked up, a big smile on his face, as he imagined Banksy with huge droopy dogs' ears and his tongue hanging out to one side looking all confused.

'We should try and practise it as soon as we can get back outside,' Tommy agreed.

'Ooh, that's weird.' Bailey picked up Alf's card from the table and studied it carefully.

'What is?' Tommy asked nervously.

'I could have sworn that this guy's face was all serious before but now he looks like he's smiling.' Bailey looked at the card, puzzled.

'I think you need my glasses.' Harry took his off and jokingly offered them to her.

'Er, yeah, I think you do,' Tommy joined in, grateful for the side swerve, and snatched the card from her hand. 'Come on, we're going to be late for class.'

Bailey looked up at Tommy quizzically. Tommy was never usually keen to get back to class.

That afternoon, Tommy put the finishing touches to his snowman. It didn't look too bad if you ignored the fact that one arm was twice the size of the other one. Tommy had been distracted all afternoon. The look on Bailey's face when she'd been looking at Alf's card had worried him. She was obviously very clever, and it would be difficult to persuade her that she was imagining things. Should he come clean and tell her all about the boots and the little shop he'd found? She would probably think he was mad.

'Thomas Green, are you with us?' Grimshaw bellowed.

Tommy looked up and saw that everyone was looking in his direction.

'Stand up and show everyone what you have made and tell us why.' Grumpy's face was all red like a tomato. Tommy had no idea what was going on, but he stood up slowly and lifted up his sock puppet.

'It's a snowman, er, because we had to,' he said.

Several children sniggered as Tommy slowly turned into a matching tomato. Grimshaw shook her head slowly from side to side, pulling a face like she'd just discovered a fly doing backstroke in her tea.

'Sit down, Thomas,' she barked.

Tommy sat down quickly.

'Harry Smith, stand up and tell us about your creation, please, and try to be a bit more interesting than Mr Green.'

That night, Tommy had Alf practise a frozen smiling pose several times just in case Bailey ever saw him again.

'Right, lad, my face is beginning to hurt, can we stop for a bit?' Alf asked.

'Yeah, all right.' Tommy sat down on his bed looking completely fed up.

'What's up, lad, can we help?' Alf asked.

'It's this stupid Christmas play. I look ridiculous, and I don't want to be in it, but my mum is all excited about coming,' Tommy explained.

'Tommy, 'ow you say, the fat lady, she no sing, no? You leave it with-a Toni, he knows what-a ta do.' Tommy watched as Toni walked off to the side of his card, leaving an empty space behind.

'Where did he go?' Tommy asked.

'I haven't the foggiest, lad,' Alf replied, fixing Tommy with a well-rehearsed frozen smile.

CHAPTER 9

A Way Out of the Manger

It had been a week since Toni had disappeared. Alf refused to tell Tommy anything more than Toni had gone to see a friend and then he would just fold his arms and fix him with his fake smile. This was why Alf had spent most of the week stuck in the drawer.

Tommy was just finishing his diary entry with a picture of Robin Banks tripping over his fake beard during the Nativity. The Nativity play was scheduled for tomorrow afternoon and Tommy did not have a single spot anywhere on his body. What he did have, however, was a school drawer full of love notes from Amber Dextrous.

'Ciao, Stanley, ciao,' came a familiar voice from Tommy's drawer.

Tommy rushed over and yanked it open. 'Toni, where have you been?' he asked hurriedly.

'Ah, Tommy, I have – 'ow you say – saved-a da day.' Toni beamed at him.

'Tommy, bedtime now, pet, big day tomorrow,' Tommy's mum called from downstairs.

'Okay, Mum,' Tommy called back.

Tommy slowly slid his drawer shut and put his PJs on. He lay in bed, wondering what Toni had been up to all week and what he'd meant by saving the day. Short of setting the school on fire, Tommy was unsure how he was going to get out of being a prehistoric sheep-man immortalised on film and humiliated for years to come.

The next day, Tommy was sitting at lunch alone. He'd avoided Bailey and Harry most days because Bailey had kept asking to see his cards again. Although he was sure Alf had got the fake smile mastered, he couldn't have shown Toni's empty card to them. Toni had shared his plan with Alf and Tommy over breakfast, whilst Tommy's mum was in the shower. Now that the play was less than an hour away, Tommy was feeling quite nervous and not overly confident that Toni's plan would work.

The Plan.

It turned out that Toni had been in Mr Ree's shop all week visiting one of the other cards, a player called Baz McAllister or 'Smasher' as he was more commonly known.

Whilst everyone was getting changed, Tommy had been told to put on his special football boots, find a red felt tip and then slip Toni's card into the headband of Banksy's costume. Whilst using Alf as a decoy, Smasher would apparently then do the rest.

Having only just met Smasher, Tommy was not convinced he would be able to stop his public humiliation, which potentially could be much worse considering he would now be a prehistoric sheep-man wearing prehistoric football boots! Still, what other choice did he have?

After lunch, the children were ushered into different classrooms to get changed. Angels in YC3P, kings in YE5O, shepherds and sheep in Tommy's classroom, WD4T, whilst Mary, Joseph and the donkey were in GO6L. Tommy had located a red felt tip easily enough, but the first real problem would be getting into GO6L.

'Mr Meener, I need the toilet,' Tommy called out.

'Quickly then, Tommy, the show's about to start and we don't have a Bo Peep.' Mr Meener chuckled to himself.

Tommy rushed through the door and found his coat peg.

He slipped on the magic boots and started to get the familiar tingling feeling. They wanted him to walk in the opposite direction of GO6L's classroom, so Tommy tried to resist and go in the opposite direction. *Stupid boots*, he thought. The boots were having none of it and instead made him walk backwards down the corridor.

'You, boy, what are you doing?' Grumpy Grimshaw bellowed behind him.

She obviously hadn't recognised who Tommy was in his costume, which didn't surprise him because he didn't look like a sheep either! Tommy turned around gingerly; this was not part of the plan.

'And what have you got on your feet?' Grimshaw walked menacingly towards him.

Suddenly, the boots started tingling like crazy and made him run towards her, causing Tommy to flail his arms about erratically as he tried to keep his balance. At the same time, his pocket started making a loud growling noise that was a cross between a barking dog and an angry gorilla. Grimshaw's face changed in an instant. She was so surprised by what she was seeing and hearing that she jumped, shrieking, into the staff toilet, locking the door behind her.

Tommy tore around the corner and instantly his feet became his own again, making him stumble to a stop. He put his hand in his pocket and fished out the culprits of the strange noises only to find Toni and Smasher now rolling around on the floor howling with laughter.

'You guys, I'm going to be in so much trouble,' Tommy whispered.

'Smasher iz funny, no?' Toni replied, wiping a tear from his cheek.

'Ganna move on, wee man, clocks a-ticking,' Smasher said, looking at Tommy whilst slowly composing himself. Smasher was a stocky blonde-haired man with a huge cheeky grin across his face. Alf had introduced Tommy to him over breakfast. He was very funny and had made Tommy laugh several times, making him spill his milky cereal all down his front.

Tommy knocked on the classroom door of GO6L and waited.

Mr Binrite opened the door and looked down at him. 'Tommy? To what do we owe this pleasure?' Mr Binrite beamed at him.

'Er, I have a message for Robin, sir,' Tommy answered.

'Righto. Robin, you have a visitor, but be quick about it, lad, we start in five minutes,' Mr Binrite said as he went back into the classroom.

Tommy's boots started tingling again and led him around the corner out of sight. He put Alf's card in the middle of the floor then hid inside a long coat that was hanging up nearby.

'Banksy, oh Banksy,' Alf called out.

Banks, at first puzzled at why there was no one at the door, heard the voice and marched towards it. Robin Banks loved football cards as much as Tommy and so Tommy knew that he would not be able to resist one just lying on the floor. Sure enough, as Banks rounded the corner, he spotted it. He looked left and right to make sure no one was looking and crouched down to scoop it up. Tommy leant out at the same time and slipped Smasher and Toni into his headband then quickly slipped back inside the coat. Banks stood up slowly, looking at the smiling player on the card, then hurriedly went back to his classroom. Tommy waited a minute then followed, making his way back to WD4T. On the way, he passed Mrs Flett, who was talking through the staff toilet door, trying to coax Grumpy Grimshaw into coming out.

'Yes, Petunia, I understand, but as you know, the children are always a bit wild around Christmas time, I'm sure it's safe to come out now, dear.'

The door opened just a crack as Tommy passed it. He

couldn't resist letting out a little growl as he went by, and the door immediately slammed shut. Tommy was grinning from ear to ear. The day was working out much better than expected.

He had just reached WD4T as everyone was filing out to take their places behind the hall curtain. Mary and Joseph were holding hands, with the donkey at the front. Mr Binrite could be heard welcoming everyone over the microphone and then he was replaced by Mr Meener's documentary-style voice over. Big Mac was in the donkey suit, which clearly didn't fit him and was causing him to fidget. Emma, who was playing Mary, looked at him crossly.

'I've acted before, so I was the obvious choice,' Bailey had overheard her saying in the playground.

Acted before? She was in a nappy advert when she was a baby, which just required her to sit and gurgle at the camera, covered in baby food! The familiar sound of 'Little Donkey' wafted through and the biblical trio disappeared into the hall. Tommy stood pensively. *Showtime*, he thought.

When Robin Banks had returned to his classroom, he'd stashed Alf's card in his drawer. What a bit of luck, he thought, it looked well old and was probably worth a fortune. He thought about it as he now looked out from his chair on stage. The things he was going to buy once he'd sold it, he thought.

'Robin, itsa wron to steal and nowza you'll be a punish,' said an eerie voice from behind him.

Banks turned quickly and looked behind him. No one was there.

'Robin, this is your conscience talking, big man, you need to hand that card back in to your teacher.'

Banks turned again towards the second voice, but no one was there.

'Yoo ava gone too far theze time and now de spritz are angry,' the first voice continued.

'Shut up!' Banks blurted out rather loudly. Emma stared

at him sternly for daring to ruin her big "journey to the stars" moment. Big Mac tried not to snigger but ended up blurting out two nostrils of snot onto Emma's hand, which made her shriek.

Smasher then shouted out, 'I'm Robin Banks and too good for this stupid play!'

Banks put his hands over his mouth instinctively, confused because, although it sounded like him, he was sure he hadn't said it.

'You're going mad, Robin, with the guilt of stealing,' Smasher continued in his ear.

Meanwhile, Emma had run off into the crowd, crying to her mum, and Big Mac was busily wiping excess snot down the front of his costume. Although Tommy couldn't see what was going on, the laughs and shrieks coming from the audience told him that things were definitely off script. Whilst the commotion was distracting everyone, Tommy slipped out the red felt tip and put red dots all over his face. He then went back to find Mrs Flett, who was now sitting on a chair outside the staff toilet telling Grumpy Grimshaw about a whale song CD she had just purchased and the wonders of seaweed wraps. Tommy was unsure whether a rap about seaweed was what Grumpy needed, but he made a mental note to check it out later.

'Mrs Flett, I don't feel too well,' Tommy said as he approached. His boots were pulling in all directions, which was causing Tommy to sway from side to side.

'Oh dear, no, you don't look well,' Mrs Flett said. 'Stay here, love, and I'll go and get your mum.'

Result! Tommy thought. Meanwhile, in the hall, it was going from bad to worse.

Smasher was now chanting, 'We're coming for you; we're coming for you,' Whilst Toni was making ghost noises. Banks was running around in hysterics whilst being chased by Mr Meener, who was desperately trying to calm him down. Mr

Binrite was at the front, claiming a slight technical hitch was responsible and that it would soon be rectified and could parents please stop filming. Mac had left the stage and was currently being wiped down by his nan with a whole packet of tissues and a bit of spit. The angels had come onto stage when the CD had moved onto 'Silent Night' and were now standing bemused by the scene that was greeting them. Mr P, who was overseeing the music, had obviously been distracted by the shenanigans and just let it play. Banks running whilst looking over his shoulder ran straight into the angels and landed in a heap of halos and legs. Emma, who had just about composed herself, then burst into tears again. Although it was currently a Welsh choir singing on the CD and not a heavy-set lady, it was safe to say the show was now over. Tommy was told to go and collect his things, ready to go home, remembering to collect Alf from Banksy's drawer first. He then made his way to the hall and found Toni and Smasher in amongst a collection of stick-on wings and tinsel.

'Come on, pet, let's get you home,' his mum said when he found her at the front door. 'You have some nasty-looking spots there, but how did you get red pen all over your face?'

Tommy, confused, looked in the car's rearview mirror when he got in the car and then at his hands. He couldn't believe it, he had really caught chicken pox!

CHAPTER 10

Food Fight

Christmas had come and gone quickly, and Tommy was now back in class with Miss Alaynious. She was covering the class because Mr Meener had gone to Thailand to find himself and Grumpy Grimshaw was on an extended spa break. Maybe she was learning to rap like Mrs Flett, Tommy thought, smiling, as he conjured up an image of Grumpy performing on stage. Today's science lesson was about melting ice. They had three ice cubes in three different beakers, of which one was wrapped in a towel, one was sitting in cold water, and one had to be held in someone's hands. Harry currently had this job as Tommy held the stopwatch. Tommy had not really enjoyed Christmas as he'd spent most of it itching, but he'd enjoyed watching his mum's video of the nativity. He hadn't seen Banksy yet because it was still wet playtimes, but he had managed to draw a ghost on the toilet wall with the message "I'm coming for you Robin" under it. He knew Banks had seen it because Bailey had told him and Harry that he had been blaming Mac in the dinner hall and that they were no longer speaking. Tommy smiled contently.

'Tom, what time you got? This cube's just a puddle now,' Harry asked, looking into the beaker.

Tommy looked at the stopwatch. Oh no, he was so busy reminiscing, he'd forgotten to start it!

'Er…' Tommy looked over at Artie and Chris's table. 'Artie, what time did you get for the one in Chris's hands?'

'Mr Green, what is the matter?' Miss Alaynious called out.

Tommy slipped the battery out of the stopwatch and held it up. 'It's not working, Miss.'

'Well, come and get another one quickly, and add the time on from someone else's,' she replied. Then she went back to her marking.

At lunch, Tommy sat with Bailey and Harry. Bailey had been right, Banks was sitting on a different table from Mackenzie and this had caused the other boys from GO6L to take sides. Leon Mee and Ally Gayter were team Mac, and Owen Cash and Si Kling were team Banks. Rohan De Boat was sitting with Emma and the other girls as she'd broken up with Robin and he was now Emma's new boyfriend. It was very hard to keep up with the BF/GF scene and Tommy was very pleased to be well clear of it. Amber Dextrous had finally stopped sending him love letters, which was lucky because he couldn't get anything else in his drawer! He had wanted to put them all in the bin, but Bailey had told him it was sweet and not to be so mean. Suddenly, an apple flew across the room and landed in Big Mac's dinner, closely followed by sniggering coming from team Banks. There was an unwritten rule in school, which was you never messed with Big Mac's dinner. Mackenzie's face turned from pink to red to purple in a matter of seconds as he tried to clean chicken curry out of his hair. Leon retaliated almost immediately, his half-eaten jam sandwich trying to make the return flight. Unfortunately, the common sandwich has very poor aerodynamics, so it had to make an emergency stop on Emma's head. Emma was now doing her best impression of a shop manikin as she froze mid-scream, hands raised either side of her head, jam slowly trickling over her left ear. Obviously, in the time-honoured fashion of chivalry, Rohan felt he should avenge Emma's dignity by sending a blueberry muffin back; well, he had been going out with her since wet play after all!

Mackenzie, being the goalkeeper that he was, caught said muffin and skilfully launched it straight into Si Kling's custard, which sent a tidal wave of yellow all over Owen

Cash. The custard was obviously hot because Cash was up like a shot doing a manic rain dance by the side of the table. Mrs White, the school dinner lady, tried desperately to intervene, but war had been declared and, within minutes of the first airstrike, a flurry of food was criss-crossing the three tables. Ally Gayter was using his spoon as a catapult, sending a steady barrage of peas from behind a stack of lunchboxes he'd pinched off a trolley. Big Mac was using his dinner tray as a cricket bat and was hitting a variety of food items back from whence they came. Many, though, were coming towards Camp Tommy, who were currently all under the table spectating with glee. Robin Banks was hiding behind Mrs White who, from the state of her, would probably have been better called Mrs Rainbow. Emma had found her voice again and was using it to good effect, as there were no visible crows in sight. Owen Cash, who had clearly cooled down, was now set up behind a chair, throwing roast potato grenades at Rohan De Boat. Rohan, who had abandoned the girls, was under a spare table, occasionally launching handfuls of pasta in every direction, hoping the scattergun approach would find a target. Si Kling had an empty lunchbox on his head and was commando-rolling all over the floor, trying in vain to dodge Leon Mee's water bottle squirt attacks.

Banks popped his head out from behind Mrs White just long enough for Tommy to bullseye him straight in the eye with a stray potato grenade.

"Ow!" Banks called out, clutching his face. Clearly disorientated, he wandered into the middle of the warzone just as Rohan's spaghetti, a half-eaten yoghurt and a doughnut flew across the room. All three missiles hit him at the same time, and he collapsed to the floor in a heap.

Bailey looked disapprovingly at Tommy who just gave a 'what did I do?' sort of shrug with a big grin on his face. Harry, though, gave him a high five.

'What on Earth is going on?!' Mr Binrite shouted as he walked into the hall, ducking a stray tomato.

Everybody stood perfectly still like they were playing musical statues, all in various mid-attack poses. Tommy struggled to stifle a snigger from under the table as the boys from GO6L were all frog-marched towards Mr Binrite's office.

CHAPTER 11
Spring Heeled

February turned out to be relatively mild weather-wise and so Mr Binrite had allowed ball games to resume at breaktimes. With Bailey on board, Harry transferred back and Big Mac now playing in goal for Tommy's team, the games had been far more even, and they had won a few. The school football team had also resumed, and Mr P had organised a friendly match after school that day against Robin Banks's club team Bowden Park, who were a mix of under tens and elevens from across the town. As a few of the school team played for Bowden Park as well, Tommy had been selected. He looked at the team sheet with Harry.

Liam Mackenzie
GK

Harry Smith   *Rohan De Boat*
CB   *CB*

Simon Kling   *Bailey Scott*   *Tommy Green*
RW   *CM*   *LW*

Leon Mee
ST

Subs:
Edward Long
Wayne Dwops
Chris Tall

'I saw Neil Downe yesterday and he said everyone from Bowden Park was playing,' Harry said gloomily.

'We are going to get destroyed,' Tommy replied, equally as glum.

Bowden Park would have Neil in goal, Ally Gayter and Davey Jones in defence. The midfield three would include Owen Cash, Banks and Jack Pott, with Jim Nasium up front.

'They have over twenty goals between them in just three school games,' Tommy said, 'look.' Tommy pointed at the league and top scorers tables.

League Table

	W	D	L	Pts	F	A	GD
All Saints	3	0	0	9	15	7	+8
Thornside	2	0	1	6	7	9	-2
Lawton	1	2	0	5	12	9	+3
Ridgeway	1	1	1	4	11	7	+4
Old Green	0	1	2	1	8	12	-4
Hawksmoor	0	0	3	0	6	15	-9

Top Goal Scorers

Jack Pott (All Saints) 9
Jim Nasium (Lawton) 9
Jaun Tu (Old Green) 7
Robin Banks (Ridgeway) 4
Leon Mee (Ridgeway) 4
Davey Jones (All Saints) 4
Markus Absent (Thornside) 3
Riley Thompson (Hawksmoor) 3

Ronny Thompson (Hawksmoor) 3
Daniel Williams (Lawton) 3
Mike Raphone (Thornside) 2
Ray Deo (All Saints) 2
Robert Smyth (Thornside) 2
Owen Cash (Ridgeway) 1
Thomas Green (Ridgeway) 1
Bailey Scott (Ridgeway) 1

Later that day, the two boys were sitting in Mr Point's classroom, this time on the floor in their positions, as Mr P practised his art on the whiteboard. Today's "visual aid" resembled a painting Tommy had been looking at in his art lesson called Number 13. It was painted by an American man called Jackson Pollock. Tommy had been interested because Jackson Pollock named lots of his work by number, just like Tommy named his corners and free kicks. He also thought it funny that a painting that looked like the floor after a WD4T art lesson could sell for thirty million pounds!

'... Then Tommy, you run in here and bish, bash, bosh, one-nil, thank you very much. All clear? Great.'

Tommy hadn't a clue what Mr P had just said, his ears had just pricked up when he heard his name. He looked over at Bailey and shrugged his shoulders. From the smile on her face, she clearly wasn't worried.

'Leon, CD player, if you please; the rest of you line up behind him.'

The team filed out and followed the music like a poor adaption of the Pied Piper up onto the pitch. The black and red nets were up, and Tommy got a familiar tingle, not in his feet but in his tummy, as he excitedly took his place. He looked over at the Bowden Park team who were kitted out in their usual black and white striped shirts with a familiar 'BEE' logo on. Looked like Mr Banks had taken his chequebook out again then.

Mr P blew his whistle and Banks shook hands with Leon. Banks won the toss and Bowden Park kicked off. This was the first time he'd played properly since his concussion and he looked raring to go. Jimbo received the ball on the halfway line and started to run down the left wing towards Si Kling. He was supported by Banks and Pott, who were both running towards goal. Kling tried to tackle Jimbo as best he could, but Jimbo performed a scissor move and sent him completely the wrong way. Jimbo was then facing Harry, who had closed the space. With a flick of his foot, Jimbo passed the ball inside towards Banks. Bailey had already anticipated this move and stole in front of him, taking the ball right from beneath his feet. With three of the Bowden Park team out of position, she sprinted with the ball into the Bowden Park half. Tommy's feet had made him run down the left wing and he was now calling for the ball. Bailey passed the ball perfectly past Owen Cash, who was trying to delay her run. Tommy's left foot caught the ball on his laces and trapped it beautifully. Davey Jones ran towards him menacingly. Tommy wanted to pass the ball to Leon Mee, but his feet began to tingle again and took over. As Jones got close, Tommy's right foot stood still on the ball. Jones tried to kick the ball from under Tommy's foot, but the magic boot pulled the ball back quickly and flicked it behind his left leg in an L shape. Tommy was now in behind the defence and didn't need his boots to tell him what to do. He ran as quickly as he could towards goal. Tommy could see Neil Downe huge in goal directly in front of him, Ally Gayter covering the space and Leon Mee, who was trying to drag Ally wider and away from goal.

'Man on,' Bailey shouted.

Banks and Pott were both closing in on him, Tommy literally had seconds to decide what to do next, but the boots made the decision for him, making him run towards Ally Gayter. By doing this, Tommy was creating space down the left-hand side. Banks and Pott were hot on his heels, Jones had recovered and had also joined the chase. Neil Downe tracked Tommy's run and moved across his goal. The right side of the pitch was now overloaded as everyone congregated around Tommy and the ball. Whilst everyone was watching Tommy, Bailey had seen the space that had been created and had run into it.

'Tommy!' she called out.

The boots made Tommy back-heel the ball straight into her path and she shot first time towards goal. Neil Downe leapt to his right and managed to parry the ball away, but Mee was first to the rebound and thumped the ball into the exposed net.

One-nil to Ridgeway.

Tommy and Harry jumped on Bailey as The Three Amigos celebrated together. Banks had a face like a bulldog chewing a wasp.

Bowden Park kicked off again but this time they were far more cautious with the ball. They kept it well and Tommy spent a lot of time pressing and being passed around. Bailey was having similar problems. Banks collected the ball near the centre spot. Bailey went to close him down, but Jack tripped her.

'Foul!' Tommy called out, but Mr P hadn't seen it.

Banks played the ball into Jimbo's feet, who flicked it with the outside of his right foot to Owen Cash. Cash expertly flip-flapped around Harry and crossed the ball left-footed high into the penalty area where Pott jumped high above Rohan and headed the ball goal-bound. Mackenzie stretched to tip it onto the crossbar but Banks, who had continued his run, got to the rebound first and tapped in for the equaliser.

One-all.

Harry helped Bailey to her feet and they both walked back to the restart. Ridgeway had not managed a single shot since they'd scored and had been well and truly outplayed. Mackenzie had made some fantastic saves to keep the score at one-all but at halftime the team looked very tired having been reduced to chasing a lot of shadows. Mr P subbed Rohan De Boat, who had not really been trying, for Chris.

'Look, guys,' Big Mac said to them all. 'I know we have not always been kind to you at school and I'm sorry for that, I am. But I want to beat Robin Banks so bad today 'cause if we don't, he will be unbearable tomorrow and you all know it. Are you with me?' he asked.

Mac put his hand out. Leon was first to put his on top, followed by Chris. Bailey looked at Harry and Tommy and put her hand in. The two boys put theirs in together. The only player who didn't was Si Kling.

'Come on, Si, we know you are Robin's mate, but surely you hate losing more?' Bailey asked him.

Si looked over at the pile of hands and expectant faces. He did like Robin, but it would be nice if he could get one over on him. He was fed up hearing about how wonderful he was and how he was getting this and that all the time.

'Yeah, okay, let's do this.' Si put his hand on top of the pile.

'Three, two, one, Ridgeway,' they all chorused.

It was a Ridgeway kick. Mr P blew the whistle and away they went.

On the way home, Tommy and Harry were in a jubilant mood. Not only had Ridgeway won, but they'd done it in style. Bailey had gone into defence and helped Harry and Mac keep Bowden Park to shooting from a distance, whilst Tommy, Si Kling, Chris and Leon passed and moved fluidly. The first goal came when Leon was tripped up by Gayter in the box. Leon took the penalty and scored. The second came from a great through ball from Bailey to Si Kling. Kling used his skills to get the better of Owen Cash and Ally Gayter and then squared the ball to Chris Tall. Chris stepped over the ball, which deceived Banks and allowed the ball to go to Tommy. Tommy's boots took over and he ran at Davey Jones. Jones, still seething from their last encounter, tried to clobber Tommy, but the boots clamped the ball together between them and jumped straight up in the air. Jones slid underneath Tommy, who was suspended momentarily in the air. When he landed, he was through on goal. Tommy was expecting to run towards Neil Downe, but the boots took a shot instead, curling the ball towards the far post. Neil Downe dived across and got a hand to it but could only push it out for a corner. Tommy ran to take it. He looked at the Bowden Park players; the size of them meant it would be pointless kicking the ball in the air as they would win it easily. Tommy put two hands in the air and hoped Harry and Bailey had remembered corner number two from their breaktime chats. Harry nodded and went towards the back post, calling Kling and Leon to join him. Banks, Pott and Jones all marked them closely, which meant the near post was clear except for Gayter and Downe. Chris Tall went and stood in front of Downe to try and block him. Jimbo stayed on the halfway line expecting Downe to catch the corner and throw it straight to him to launch a counterattack. Bailey silently crept away from him on his blind side until she was far enough away and then she ran, and boy could she run. Jimbo caught a glimpse of her from the corner of his eye and gave chase, but it was too late, she was ahead of him.

'Watch her!' he called out.

Tommy timed his pass perfectly so that Bailey didn't have to break her stride and she shaped to shoot. Gayter moved across to block her but, instead of shooting like Tommy had shown her, she faked the shot and slipped it through Gayter's open legs. She then side-stepped Ally and collected the ball on her favoured right foot, smashing it low and hard across goal. Downe managed to get a long leg past Chris to deflect the shot towards the gathered masses on the far post. Tommy had followed his pass and was running into the box as he watched the scramble to get to the rebound first. It was Kling who made it. He fired a first time shot back across goal. Downe was still stranded on the floor and could do nothing to stop Tommy arriving to tap it in from just three feet.

Final score three-one Ridgeway.

The boys stood panting at the third lamppost on Granville Street.

'See you tomorrow, Haz,' Tommy called out as he swung into his gate.

'See you later, Tom,' Harry replied.

Tommy ran up the stairs two at a time. He was buzzing from head to toe. He went to his drawer and chatted to Alf and Toni for at least the next hour, replaying every kick for them in detail. After his tea, he wrote his diary entry for the day.

I hate Robin Banks. Today was a great day, though, as Ridgeway beat Bowden Park three-one. Banks was so angry, he didn't shake anyone's hand after the game; instead, he stormed off in a huff. I can't wait until school tomorrow. He won't be so smug now.

Tommy finished his entry with a picture of himself jumping high in the air with the ball between his feet, Davey Jones sliding beneath him.

CHAPTER 12
United We Stand

It had been a week since the friendly with Bowden Park. Robin Banks had ignored everyone at school except for Emma Nently, who was now his girlfriend again because he had restarted training with United. Tommy hadn't minded, though, as Banks had left him well alone and had not played in any of the breaktime battles. Harry and Tommy had arranged to meet Bailey in the corridor to check the team sheet for the next league match against Old Green – Jaun Tu's team. They found her looking pensively at the board.

'Hey, Bailey, what's up?' Tommy asked.

'Tommy, you and Harry have been dropped,' she replied, anger etched in her face. 'What is Mr P thinking?'

Tommy and Harry looked at the board. Sure enough, they'd been replaced and the original school lineup from the seven-two win over Thornside had been chosen with the addition of Bailey on the bench. Whilst Tommy accepted this team had recorded their best result of the season so far against Thornside, he thought that he and Harry had done enough to warrant a place on the bench, at least. Instead, Wayne Dwops and Edward Long had been chosen over them. Ed Long, really? What had he actually done except go to the toilet?

'What's the matter, Green? You didn't seriously think you were going to get selected when Si and I were fit, did you?' Banks hollered down the corridor.

'Leave him alone, Robin, I'd rather have him and Smithy in the team over Ed Long any day,' Kling defended them.

'Are you winding me up, Si? I'd rather have Mrs White play than that squirt,' Banks retorted.

'What was the score last week, Banksy?' Bailey asked. 'I'm surprised that Mr P has selected you after how poor you were. Guess Daddy's chequebook bought you a spot then.'

Banks looked like he was going to erupt as he strode towards her, fists clenched. He was nearly close enough to touch her when suddenly Big Mac stepped in between them.

'You got a problem with Bailey, Banks, then you have a problem with me,' he said, looking down at the smaller boy.

'And me,' called out Leon as he joined Big Mac's side.

'And me,' echoed Gayter as he joined Mac's other side.

Banks looked at the three of them and slowly shook his head.

'Can't you see what they're doing to us, lads? We won't win the league this way. We need to stick together. We are a team, a good team,' Banks preached.

Then he turned and walked away, shaking his head.

'I'll be seeing you soon, Scotty,' he called out over his shoulder.

The day of the football match against Old Green arrived. Mr Nomos had mowed the grass and freshly painted the lines. The red and black corner flags were in place, flapping in the wind, giving the optical illusion that the bee in the centre was being electrocuted. The custom red-and-black-striped nets were up, and Harry and Tommy were in their usual spot at the top of the climbing frame. Tommy put his coat over the bars, took his juice bottle out, balancing it carefully on the corner where the two poles joined, like he'd done so many times before, and sighed.

'What's up, mate?' Harry asked, although he knew perfectly well because he felt the same.

'It just feels so unfair, Haz, we should both be in Mr

Point's room right now getting confused trying to decipher his scribbling,' Tommy replied sadly.

Harry was just about to speak when suddenly the familiar sound of Italian opera music washed across the field, Banks at the front of the line of marching red-and-black-shirted boys and Bailey, hair immaculate as always, boots freshly polished, CD player in his left hand, match ball under his right arm. Instead of trying to ridicule the procession, though, Tommy was left feeling green with envy. The Ridgeway team started their warmup. Bailey looked over and waved at them both. The boys waved back.

In the car park, the Old Green spectators and players had started to arrive. Old Green were in their usual green-and-white-hooped shirts, white shorts and green socks. Jaun Tu was wearing the captain's armband and was juggling a football by the goal nearest the boys.

'He's good, isn't he, Tommy,' Harry said.

'Yep, looks like Neil was right, he hasn't dropped the ball once yet,' Tommy replied.

Mr P blew the whistle and Banks shook hands with Tu. Banks won the toss of the coin and chose to kick off first. Leon passed the ball back to Banks, who flicked it up and started ball juggling. Jaun Tu ran towards him, and Banks flipped the ball over his head.

'Olé!' Banks called out as the ball went over Tu's head. Tu just calmly flicked his foot out backwards and used his heel to flick the ball back over his own head and towards the Ridgeway goal.

'Olé!' he replied and ran after the ball.

Rohan and Ally both ran towards Tu, but he span on top of the ball and passed straight through the middle of them. Mackenzie rushed out to close him down but Tu just calmly rainbow-flicked the ball over him into the goal.

'Whoa!' Tommy exclaimed.

102

Harry just whistled.

Tommy looked down at Bailey, who just had her head in her hands. Banks was such a show-off and now the must-win game had become that little bit harder. Ridgeway kicked off again. This time Banks was not in such a hurry to show off, instead passing the ball out to Si on the right wing, who immediately attacked the Old Green left back, Frank Furter, at speed. Jaun Tu chased after him, but Kling passed the ball into Leon Mee, who shot first time. The ball flew at speed, goal-bound, but hit the post. The goalkeeper tried to kick it clear but passed it straight to Owen Cash who calmly slotted the ball home.

One-all, game on.

Jaun Tu collected the ball and went to the centre circle. Mr P blew the whistle and Tu shot straight from the centre. Mackenzie was well off his line and the ball sailed over him into the top corner. Tu looked straight at Banks.

'Olé!' he goaded.

Tommy looked at Harry, both speechless.

Banks grabbed the ball from Leon and waited for Mr P to blow the whistle. As soon as the whistle went, Banks tried to do the same as Tu and score from the centre, except his shot went narrowly wide. Tu smirked and pretended to rub his eyes like he was crying. Banks was being played but he couldn't see it.

The game ebbed and flowed, Banks making lots of mistakes as Tu continued to wind him up. Bailey had been told to warm up as Mr P tried to work out how to contain the influential Tu. She came on for De Boat as the team switched to a one-four-one system with Bailey playing inside with Banks. Her first touch was on the edge of the Old Green box. She intercepted a goal kick and shaped to shoot. Tu got his body in the way to block her shot, but it was a fake to draw him out of position. Instead of shooting, she rolled the ball across the edge of the box for Si Kling to shoot near-post. The shot was hit too hard for the keeper to stop it.

Two-all at halftime.

Harry and Tommy couldn't hear what was being said from on the top of the climbing frame, but from the look of the jumping around and all the arm waving, Mr P was clearly very excited. Bailey, on the other hand, looked confused, especially when Leon and Ally were swapped for Ed and Wayne. Behind them, Artie and Chris had climbed up to join them for the second half.

'All right, lads,' Artie called out. 'Good game, innit?'

'Yeah,' replied Tommy. 'Jaun Tu is quality.'

'I like the way he's winding up Banksy,' Chris sniggered.

The other three agreed and chuckled as they tuned in for the second half.

It was an Old Green centre. Tu passed the ball back to his teammates and the game began. Ridgeway were playing a three-two-one formation now with Dwops, Long and Kling in defence, Bailey and Banks in the middle and Cash up front.

Tu picked the ball up again and started to dribble towards the Ridgeway half. Cash tried to tackle him first, but Tu just waltzed past him. Banks was next. He flew at him, still seething at being humiliated in the first half. Tu just dropped his shoulder and side-stepped him easily. Bailey was next. *She won't be so easy*, Tommy thought, but Tu didn't even try. Instead, he smashed the ball straight at Edward Long, which hit him in the stomach and made him fall over. Tu ran past Bailey and collected the spilt ball. Wayne Dwops ran over to try and intercept, but he was too far away, and Tu had more than enough time to pull the trigger. His shot was low and hard this time, making Mackenzie dive low. Mac got his right hand to it and managed to stop the ball going in, but Tu had reacted the quickest and, with Mackenzie now on the floor, he calmly did a Rabona over the stricken keeper. Tu then stepped over Mac and picked the ball up from out of the net. He carried the ball over to Banks and gave it to him.

'Olé!' he laughed.

Three-two to Old Green.

Mr Point was helping Ed Long get up and trying to stop his mum from running onto the pitch with a packet of baby wipes. Bailey had called the other players over into a huddle. Tommy was desperate to hear what she was saying, so he scrambled down the climbing frame and ran to the edge of the pitch where Ally, Rohan and Leon were standing.

'… the place and can't continue like this because we will lose. Robin, do you think that United would be impressed with the way you're playing? You have got to leave Tu alone and concentrate on your own game. We all know you're a good player, but you're not showing it today. Mr P means well but he's got us all running around in circles just like the ones he draws on the board. We need to play like we do at breaktimes and just enjoy ourselves. We cannot do this on our own, though, we need to do it together, as a team. Are you with me?' Bailey asked the group.

It was a great speech, Tommy thought, and she was exactly right, of course. Tommy was not really sure what the warm feeling was inside him, but this wasn't the first time he'd felt it when he'd listened to Bailey speak. Banks pulled his armband off and held it out towards Bailey. Everyone stood there open-mouthed as he offered it to her. Could Robin Banks really be accepting Bailey was the better captain? Bailey put her hand out to take it gratefully but, just as she nearly touched it, Banks snatched it back.

'In your dreams, Scott!' Banks sneered. 'If you put as much effort into playing as you do talking rubbish then we might just stand a chance. Just give me and Owen the ball and we'll do the rest. Oh, and Mac, do you think you could save a couple of shots this half, yeah?'

He and Owen walked off laughing. Mac was fuming and wanted to go after them, but Bailey stepped in front of him.

'Ignore him, Liam,' she said.

Liam! That's brave, Tommy thought. Only his mum and the teachers called him Liam. He didn't seem bothered, though, because he nodded and made his way back to goal.

'Gayter!' Mr P called out. 'You're back on. Edward's mum is taking him to casualty.'

He needs to take Banks off, Tommy thought. Ridgeway kicked off, Cash playing the ball to Banks, who then tried to dribble around the whole Old Green team. To be fair, he got around the first three players easily, but then Tu was in his way. He was going to lose the ball again Tommy thought, but before Banks had the chance to try and show off, Bailey skipped in front of him and stole the ball. She then passed the ball back to Ally in defence. Tu chased the backwards pass, as she knew he would. Bailey then made a forward run, expecting the long ball over the top. Ally did not disappoint, as he smashed it high over Tu's head. Bailey watched the ball over her shoulder, turning at exactly the right second to control the ball on her thigh. She then turned and ran towards goal. Owen Cash was running down the left wing calling for the ball, Si Kling down the right. Without Tu in their way, the Ridgeway players were able to attack the space freely. Bailey chose to pass the ball to Kling, who cut inside onto his left foot and shot low at the far post. The Old Green keeper couldn't reach the ball and it nestled into the bottom corner.

Three-all.

'YES!' shouted Tommy, who was now back at the top of the climbing frame with the others.

Kling, Gayter, Dwops and Big Mac all ran over to Bailey and gave her a high five. Banks, on the other hand, was talking to Mr Point.

'Leon, Rohan, you're on,' Mr P called over to the bench. 'Bailey, Wayne, off you go.'

'What!' Harry and Tommy exclaimed at the same time.

'Bailey is the only reason we are still in the game, Tom,' said Harry.

'Yeah, I know,' Tommy replied. 'Banks must have said something to Mr Point.'

'He is so selfish,' exclaimed Artie. 'He can't stand it when others get the praise.'

'He will lose us the game at this rate,' Chris agreed.

Tu restarted the game. At least with the players that were on, Ridgeway would be playing a more balanced two-three-one formation. With Banks and Tu constantly trying to outskill each other, the game became very stale, and the time ticked on.

'Ridgeway need to win this game, Harry, otherwise we won't have a chance of winning the league this year,' Tommy said.

'Not if Lawton and All Saints keep winning, we won't,' agreed Harry.

'Fortunately, they still have to play each other, so hopefully they will draw, and both drop points,' observed Tommy.

Bailey sat stewing under a cloud with Wayne Dwops on the sidelines as she watched Banks pretty much play by himself. *Did United really think he was any good?* she thought to herself. Owen Cash picked up the ball on a rare occasion that Banks and Tu were not hogging it. He started to run down the left wing, cutting inside so he could shoot, but Frank Furter ran into him, causing him to fall just outside the penalty area.

'Ow!' came a cry from Cash.

'Looks like he's twisted his ankle, Tom,' Harry said.

'Yeah, hopefully Bailey will get back on now,' replied Tommy.

'Wayne, you're on, Cash can't continue,' called out Mr P.

Tommy put his head in his hands and sighed.

'Look, Tommy, Wayne is refusing to go on and Bailey is going on instead.'

Tommy's head snapped up. *Thank goodness*, Tommy thought, *but why is Wayne not going on?*

It was a free kick to Ridgeway. Banks was standing over it because he always took the free kicks and the penalties when he was playing. Old Green set up a three-man wall with Tu on the left-hand side of it. Bailey was talking to Leon and Si and then she went over to Banksy. Tommy wished he knew what she was saying to him. He loved listening to her talk about football.

'Whoa, Tommy, look, Banks is letting Bailey take the free kick,' Harry exclaimed.

Harry was right, Banks was standing near Tu now and Bailey was on the ball. Mee and Kling were behind her, and Ally Gayter was standing opposite the back post, pulling a defender out of position. Mr Point blew the whistle and Banks ran in front of the wall screaming for Bailey to pass to him. Bailey ran towards the ball and shaped to pass the ball to him. Tu had seen what was happening and chased after Banks, leaving a hole in the wall. At the same time, Leon Mee ran behind Bailey through the new hole and Bailey ran over the ball, leaving it for Si Kling to pass the ball to Leon.

'It's Fetch, Harry!' Tommy blurted out. 'Artie, Chris, watch this. If it works, it'll be brilliant.'

Tommy was right. Mee was now through on goal because the wall had all followed Banksy's run. Mee shot low and hard, but the ball hit the post and ricocheted straight in front of Banks, who smashed it in from close range. Banks then ran the full length of the pitch, whooping and hollering like he'd just scored the winning goal in the World Cup final.

'Look at him, Haz. That goal was as much Leon's as it was

his and yet he's making out it's all down to him. Can you see why I can't stand him?' Tommy seethed.

'Yeah, I know, Tom, I know,' replied Harry.

The rest of the team were all around Bailey, patting her on the back for her free-kick routine. Old Green kicked off but there was not enough time left for them to get back into the game. Mr P blew the final whistle.

Final score: Four-three to Ridgeway.

Tommy watched as Bailey went over to Jaun Tu to shake his hand. Tommy could see the mutual respect between them. Banks, however, was nowhere to be seen.

On the way home, Tommy and Harry chatted excitedly about Bailey's free-kick routine. It had turned out Wayne had not wanted to go back on because he knew Bailey was their best chance of winning. Instead, he'd told Mr Point his leg was hurting.

'It worked so well, didn't it, Harry? Old Green were completely duped, including Tu. Bailey is just brilliant,' Tommy said wistfully.

'So was Tu, though, wasn't he?' Harry asked.

'Yeah, Neil Downe wasn't wrong. That rainbow-flick goal was awesome,' Tommy agreed.

'Makes you wonder why United haven't asked him for a trial. He was better than Banks tonight,' stated Harry.

'So was Bailey,' replied Tommy.

'I think you fancy Bailey, Tom,' Harry chided.

'No, I don't,' he retorted, quickly blushing.

'I think she likes you too, mate. Look, she's followed us home.' Harry pointed behind them.

Tommy turned and looked down the street. There was nobody there. He turned back to ask Harry what he was on about, but Harry was running flat out to the corner of Granville Street.

'You little cheat!' Tommy called after him, immediately

breaking into a sprint of his own, a huge grin on his face.

Tommy was gaining on Harry by the first lamppost. By the second, he could almost touch him. One lamppost to go. Tommy dropped his bag and ran at full speed. He was not ready to let his gold medal go just yet. Harry being the bigger boy had a much longer running stride, but Tommy was much lighter and more nimble. It was going to be close. Five metres, three metres, one...

Tommy lay on his bed upstairs thinking about the day. He had told his mum, Alf, Toni and his diary all about it. With Ridgeway getting three points tonight, they had an outside chance of winning the league, but a lot would depend on tomorrow's game between Lawton and All Saints. If All Saints won, they would have twelve points and Ridgeway would not be able to catch them. Tommy thought about this as he drifted off to sleep.

The next day at school, Tommy, Bailey and Harry were in the lunch hall talking about last night's game.

'Fetch worked so well, Bailey, but how did you get Banks to agree to letting you take it?' Tommy asked.

'Easy,' she said. 'I told him that the little man in the crowd with the funny red hat was a Reds scout and that I would pass the ball straight to him so he could score. Even though he is trialling for United, his ego couldn't resist wanting another club to be after him.'

'What little man?' Tommy asked, guessing the answer already.

'I dunno. I think he was an Old Green player's grandad, but he had this strange red hat on that looked like a lamp shade,' Bailey answered.

Tommy looked confused. Why was Mr Ree at the game? Tommy wasn't even playing!

'What's up, Tom, are you still worried that I nearly beat you last night by saying…?'

Tommy cut Harry off. 'Don't you dare, Haz.'

'What did you say, Harry?' Bailey asked.

Harry looked at Tommy, whose face was ashen.

'I told him… his shoes were untied,' Harry lied, laughing.

'Oh, Tommy, you didn't fall for that, did you?' Bailey laughed.

Tommy sighed with a sense of relief. He didn't really think Harry would say anything, but he'd still felt panicked at the thought of Bailey knowing he liked her.

CHAPTER 13

By the Skin of Their Teeth

After school that night, The Three Amigos walked across town to Lawton primary school so they could watch the big game against All Saints. Harry's dad had said he would collect them at 4.45pm and drive them all home afterwards. The Lawton pitch was tiny compared to the Ridgeway's and this was one of the reasons why Jimbo scored so many goals. You could score from goal kicks the goals were so close. The three friends found a place to sit by the side of the pitch.

'Hey, Tommy, Hazza, can I sit with you guys?'

Tommy looked up to see Neil Downe walking over.

'Yeah, course,' Tommy replied, motioning to the others to move up.

'Hi, I'm Neil,' the tall boy said to Bailey.

'Um, I'm, er...' she stammered.

'This is Bailey,' Harry laughed.

Bailey was blushing. 'Look, er, Lawton are coming out,' she deflected.

Jimbo was at the front of the line, match ball under his arm.

'I hope he's got his shooting boots on,' Tommy said, looking at Bailey and wondering why she was behaving so oddly. 'Why have you come to watch, Neil?'

'We are playing them here next week,' he replied. 'I wanted to watch them play because we have an outside chance of winning the league, same as you. Our schools are both on seven points each now.'

'What was your score last night then?' Harry asked.

'We drew with Hawksmoor two-all,' replied Neil.

'We've got to play Hawksmoor next week,' Tommy said. 'How did the Thompson twins play?'

'They both got one a-piece again last night. Do you know they've both scored once each in every game so far?' asked Neil.

'Yeah, Mr Point puts a goal scoring list up at school,' answered Tommy.

Both teams were now out and lining up, ready for kick off. Jack Pott had won the toss and was standing over the ball. The whistle went and Pott played the ball backwards towards Davey Jones. Jimbo chased the ball down quickly. Because the pitch was so short, Jones had very little space to play around him and misplaced a pass to the keeper. Jimbo intercepted the ball and placed the ball into the net.

One-nil to Lawton.

'Wow, great start,' Tommy said.

All Saints kicked off again, but this time Pott was not looking to play backwards. He played a quick one-two with his right midfielder and ran towards the Lawton left back. Jimbo tried to tackle him, but Pott pushed him away with his strength. Even though they were teammates at Bowden Park, there would be no love lost in this match. Both were desperate to win the league for their schools and would give everything. Pott took a shot, but hit the crossbar. Lawton regained the ball and knocked it long. Davey Jones headed the ball back the way it had come but straight to Jimbo, who volleyed the ball first time, but the ball sailed narrowly wide.

'This is more like tennis than football,' Bailey remarked.

'Do you like tennis?' Neil asked. 'We can have a game sometime if you like?'

Bailey just looked at him wide-eyed. 'Er...'

'She can't,' Tommy blurted out. 'She's not got a racket.

Look, Jack Pott is through on goal,' he said, quickly changing the subject.

Sure enough, Jack was in the box clear of the defence. He absolutely smashed the ball straight into the top corner of the net so hard that the goal lifted off the ground slightly.

One-all.

Bailey was looking at Tommy. 'How do you know I don't have a racket?' she asked him.

'Lucky guess?' Tommy shrugged.

Bailey fixed Tommy with a stern look that made him feel a little uncomfortable. 'For your information, I do have a racket, thank you very much.'

'You don't use it, though, do you?' Tommy replied, a little scared.

'I'll have you know, Tommy Green, I play a lot and I'm pretty good, actually!' Bailey had now put her hands on her hips as well.

Tommy wished the floor would open up and swallow him. It didn't, but the next best thing happened – Jack Pott had just scored again.

'Oh no,' moaned Harry. 'What was the keeper doing?'

'I guess he wasn't ready for the Pott shot,' Neil quipped.

The others all groaned but smiled and Tommy was grateful for the deflection.

Although Tommy was worried that All Saints were now in the lead and on course to win the league, he was also relieved that Bailey had seemingly forgotten their awkward conversation and was now focused back on the game. Danny 'The Tank' Williams of Lawton played the ball short to Jimbo, who clipped the ball with the outside of his right foot making it swerve around the outstretched hand of the keeper and hit the post. Davey Jones collected the rebound and ran into the Lawton half, only to be tackled and lose the ball again near the centre circle. Williams had regained the ball and passed it back to Jimbo, who shot first time and equalised.

Two-all.

The score kept going up and up and, by halftime, Lawton were trailing six-four. Tommy had not spoken again since he and Bailey had discussed her tennis abilities.

'It's gonna be close,' Harry announced obviously to the group.

'I think All Saints are too strong for them,' Neil said. 'What do you think, Tommy?'

'I'm not sure,' he replied. 'Jimbo is playing well but Tank is struggling to stop Jack Pott. It could still go either way.'

'Look, Tank Williams is going off but who is that coming on?' Harry asked.

'Dunno,' Neil said. 'He must be new.'

A small, dark-haired boy walked over to the centre circle with Jimbo. He had dark olive skin and long, black, curly hair. Although he was small, he looked very strong. Jimbo kicked him the ball and then he was off. The ball looked like it was glued to his feet. The first All Saints player he encountered offered no resistance as the new boy calmly tapped the ball through his legs. The next player he met was no different. The boy stepped over the ball four times very quickly, which caused the defender to fall over backwards.

'Diego!' Jimbo called out as he ran to the edge of the All Saints penalty area.

Jack Pott was Diego's next opponent. Jack tried hard to knock him off the ball using his strength, but Diego didn't move, he dropped his shoulder and rolled the ball through Pott's legs. Jack turned quickly to give chase, but Diego back-heeled the ball back through Pott's legs again. Tommy, Harry, Neil and Bailey sat watching opened-mouthed. With Pott twisted inside out, Diego crossed the ball expertly towards the penalty spot. Jimbo and Jones both ran to get to the ball first. Jimbo was the quicker of the two boys. Using his body to shield Jones from getting to the ball, he half turned away from the goal and leapt up in the air, twisting perfectly to bicycle-kick the ball into the top bin.

Six-five to All Saints.

'Whoa,' the four friends said in unison.

Diego casually collected the ball and placed it on the centre spot. Jones and Potts were shaking their heads in disbelief.

'Thank goodness Diego didn't play against us, Tommy,' Bailey said.

'I know, right, he's quality. Where did he come from, I wonder?' he replied.

'Banksy would still say he was better, though,' Neil quipped.

The four friends were still laughing as Diego stole the ball off Jack Pott's feet in the middle of the pitch and then he was off. He skipped past the All Saints players easily, changing direction too quickly for them. Diego was also lightning fast, but the ball never left his left foot, his control was exceptional.

'Put him in your locker, Davey,' his dad shouted out again.

'Does he ever say anything else?' Harry asked.

Tommy was not sure what sort of locker Davey Jones was hoping to use, but unless it had three miles of chain and barbed wire wrapped around it, he was doubtful it would contain Diego. Tommy was right. Jones approached him side on but was being far too cautious, trying to delay Diego instead so that Jack Pott could make a recovery run to help. With all the space left in front of Diego, he attacked Davey head on. First, he rolled the ball with his right foot across his body, then he flip-flapped the ball with his left so that he was now on the touchline, goal on his inside. Jones fell for the bait and came in closer, expecting to force Diego out of play. Diego rolled the ball backwards on top of his left foot and then scooped the ball up and over Davey's head. Diego ran around on the inside catching the ball before it touched the floor on his right foot. He pushed the ball forwards and accelerated fast towards goal. Jimbo was making a run through the middle of the pitch, Pott hot on his heels.

'Diego!' Jimbo called out.

Tommy watched as Diego did a Rabona with his left foot. The ball arched high over the other Saints defender and dropped right in front of Jim Nasium. Jimbo didn't miss chances like this, and he didn't disappoint. He coolly placed the ball to the keeper's left with too much pace for him.

Six-all.

Jack Pott looked deflated. Diego was proving impossible to stop. He passed the ball to the All Saints right winger, Ray Deo, who was obviously not ready to give in. He ran at the Lawton defence in defiance and shot at goal, but the ball sailed wide. The game ebbed and flowed with shots firing off from both teams regularly, but with only eight minutes left, it was still tied at six-all. If All Saints could keep it a draw, they would only need a point against Old Green next week to win the league. Therefore, they had resorted to sitting back in their own half and shooting from a distance. Because the pitch was so small, Lawton were struggling for space and were shooting from much further back. Davey Jones received the ball from a goal kick and ran forwards. Jimbo closed him down, forcing him to play the ball inside to Pott. Jack had Diego in front of him. Knowing he would struggle to dribble past him, he chose to shoot instead and thumped the ball towards the goal. *That's in*, Tommy thought. The ball flew through the air and hit the underside of the crossbar, bouncing down over the line.

Seven-six to All Saints. Five minutes to go.

'Oh no,' Neil Downe sighed.

Lawton kicked off and tried to attack but All Saints were

even more camped in than before. Jack Pott was sitting back in defence now with Davey Jones. They knew if they could hold off Lawton for the next few minutes, they had won the league. Diego collected the ball to the left side of the centre circle, a wall of All Saints players in front of him. He had a huge smile on his face. *Does he realise he's losing?* Tommy thought. Diego flicked the ball up with his left foot and started to juggle with the ball. He flipped the ball from his foot to his thigh back to his foot and then up to his shoulder. Ray Deo of All Saints, frustrated by Diego's showboating, broke ranks and tried to tackle him. This was a mistake. Diego flicked the ball onto the back of his neck and then span around quickly, which caused the ball to 360 with him. Ray ran straight through the empty space like he had run through a revolving door. Tristan Shout, another All Saints player, tried to tackle him, but this time Diego nutmegged him and waltzed around the other side. Five players now stood in his way. Jimbo ran round the back of Diego and called for the ball. Diego obliged and then ran in the opposite direction towards where Jack and Jones were camped on the edge of their box. Nasium skipped past the All Saints midfield and passed the ball back to Diego, who had just arrived in front of Pott. Instead of trapping the ball, he ran over it and let the ball continue rolling into the penalty area. Pott fell for the feint and followed Diego instead of the ball. This allowed Diego to get in behind Pott and Jones with just the keeper to beat. The Saints keeper rushed off his line in the hope he could get there first, but Diego was too quick, and he poked the ball past him. Diego lined up his foot to tap the ball into the empty net, but Davey Jones went straight through the back of him. Diego rolled over, clutching the back of his left leg, clearly hurt.

'Penalty,' the referee announced and pointed to the spot.

Diego had been substituted, unable to carry on. Danny

Williams came back on as Jimbo collected the ball and placed it on the spot.

'Come on, Jimbo,' Tommy said softly to himself, crossing his fingers.

Jimbo walked back a few paces and got set. The whistle blew. He started his run up and kicked the ball hard with his laces. Tommy held his breath. The ball hit the keeper's leg and struck the post, but Jimbo got to the rebound the quickest and thumped it in, making no mistake this time.

Seven-all. Two minutes left.

Pott kicked the ball back to Jones and Jimbo desperately chased after it. Jones wasn't going to get caught again, though, and just smashed the ball back up field. Tank collected the ball on his chest and passed to Jim Nasium, who had dropped deep to collect it. The clock was winding down and the Saints were in no hurry to press him. Jimbo was a good player but so were Jack and Jones. Without Diego to help him, Tommy was sure the game was destined for a draw. Just then, Tank Williams made a driving run through the middle of the pitch, Jimbo passed him the ball and Tank powered forward. Jack challenged him hard and the two boys both hit the floor.

'Play on,' called out the referee.

Jimbo chased the loose ball and so did Davey Jones. Jimbo was quick but Jones was closer to the ball. *Come on, Jimbo,* Tommy willed him silently, fists clenched in anticipation. Jones reached the ball a whisker before Nasium and tried to smash it away, but Jimbo blocked his clearance and the ball deflected off his knee towards the All Saints goal. Tank was already back on his feet and chased after the stray ball. Jack was right behind him, desperately trying to get in front. The All Saints keeper was off his line, coming out to catch the aerial ball. Tank jumped up to meet the ball with his head just as the keeper arrived, trying to punch the ball clear. Tank reached the ball first and headed the ball goal-bound. Jack kept running and very nearly saved the ball off the line, but he wasn't quite quick enough, and the ball crossed the line.

Eight-seven to Lawton. Sixty seconds left.

Jack and Jones were both at the centre talking. Pott took a few steps backwards and Jones stood by the ball.

'He's going to shoot,' Tommy said.

The four of them watched agog. Sure enough, Jones played the ball slightly forward and Pott ran and hammered the ball for goal. Tommy's mouth dropped; it was on target. Tank tried to head it clear, but it was too high for him. The Lawton keeper put his hands up to save the ball but mistimed his catch and took the full weight of the ball straight in the face. Williams collected the loose ball and thumped it back up the other way. Jimbo sprinted after it, but the whistle blew. The Lawton keeper was still down. He had lost a tooth! Tank Williams swapped jerseys and went in goal, as the Lawton keeper went off to a hero's applause. Lawton only had six players on the pitch with just under a minute to go. The referee restarted with a drop ball, Jack and Jimbo contesting. What a game it had been. Pott won the drop ball and flicked it to Jones. Jimbo pressed him quickly, but Jones passed the ball forwards to an All Saints winger who was free. Pott ran into the Lawton half screaming for the ball. The ball was played beautifully in front of him, and he unleashed a powerful shot at goal. Williams managed to get a hand to the ball and deflect it onto the crossbar. The ball dropped and fell towards the goal line. Tommy stared, mouth open wide. The ball bounced on the line, but Williams scooped it up into his arms and lay still, cradling the ball as the final whistle blew.

Tommy breathed out, 'Wow, what a game.'

They had found Harry's dad in the car park and Neil had hitched a ride home with them. They'd dropped Bailey off first, not far from Maurice Road, and then pulled the car up outside Harry's house. Tommy, Harry and Neil all jumped out.

'Thanks, Mr Smith,' Tommy said as Harry and his dad went inside.

'See you tomorrow, Tommy,' Harry called back.

'How good was Diego?' Neil asked.

'Yeah, he was awesome,' Tommy agreed. 'You're going to need magic gloves to stop him next week.'

Neil laughed and started walking up the road. Magic gloves, magic gloves! Tommy's mind was racing. Was it possible?

'Oh, Tommy,' Neil called out, turning around. 'Does Bailey have a boyfriend?'

Tommy froze for a second, then stammered, 'Yeah... sorry... and um, he's really big.'

'Shame,' Neil said, turning back around and walking away.

Really big?! Look at the size of Neil Downe, how much bigger could you get? Tommy had regretted saying it almost immediately. Why had he lied? What would Bailey say if she found out he'd lied? Look at the way she'd reacted when he'd said she didn't have a tennis racket. Oh, what a mess. Why were girls so complicated? Tommy went inside and was greeted by the smell of food cooking.

'Hi, Mum,' he called out.

'Hiya, pet, did you have a nice day?' she replied. 'Go get changed and I'll call you down when yer tea's ready.'

Tommy ran upstairs and changed into his Red's replica kit. He opened his drawer and took out Alf and Toni. He placed them in his dad's old wallet and stood it up on the carpet.

'... then Diego span around and put the ball through the next player's legs,' Tommy was explaining.

'Ee sounz lika me when I woz a-younger,' Toni said.

'He sounds like he could be better than you, Toni lad,' Alf responded.

'No, eez not possible,' Toni retorted, putting his nose in the air.

Tommy laughed.

'Tea's ready, pet,' Mrs Green called from the kitchen.

CHAPTER 14

A Helping Hand

The next day, Tommy and Harry were sitting in assembly. Mr Binrite was reminding everybody that the permission slips for the upcoming school trip to the zoo needed to be in before the end of next week. 'Make sure that you hand them in to your teacher as soon as possible, please. Right, finally: as you are aware, our school football captain, Robin Banks, has been trialling with United over the last few weeks and it is my absolute pleasure to announce that he has been signed on a two-year contract. Come on up, lad, come on up.'

Tommy looked at Harry then he scanned for Bailey. Bailey pulled a face and shook her head in disbelief.

'So, Robin, what does this mean?' Mr Binrite asked.

'Well, it means I can't play for Bowden Park anymore because I'm a United under-eleven's player now. Instead of playing against amateurs each week, I'll be playing against teams like the Reds and the Blues instead,' Banks boasted.

'You can still play for the school, though, is that correct?' Mr Binrite asked.

'Yes, I can, but my dad says I shouldn't,' Robin replied.

'Why is that, Robin?' Mr Binrite asked nervously.

'Because he says that everyone will be jealous of me and try and kick me. He doesn't want me to get injured playing against rubbish players as I'm too good to be playing at this level,' Banks gloated.

A boo came from behind Tommy. Tommy turned just in time to see Big Mac cupping his hand to his mouth and sniggering.

'Right, right, sit down, boy, sit down,' Mr Binrite said, ushering him back towards his class, clearly flustered.

Tommy looked over at Mr Point who was sitting with his head in his hands. No Owen Cash, who had sprained an ankle in the match against Old Green, and now no Banks. Next week's game against Hawksmoor was a must-win if they were to have any chance of winning the league and now two of their best players weren't available for selection. Tommy felt Mr P's pain, but also realised this meant he might be chosen to play again.

After assembly, Tommy ran to the corridor to check out the updated league table. Bailey was already there.

'There are four teams that can still win this, Tommy,' Bailey said as he approached. 'Thornside have got to play Lawton, All Saints have got to play Old Green and we've got Hawksmoor.'

'Yeah, I know. If Lawton or All Saints win their games, we won't be able to win the league, even if we beat Hawksmoor next week,' Tommy replied.

'That won't be easy, either, with Banks and Cash both out,' Bailey observed.

'A lot will depend on who Mr P picks to play for us,' Tommy said.

'You're right, Tom, he'd better pick you and Harry,' Bailey agreed.

Will Neil Downe be able to stop Diego and Jimbo, though? Tommy thought as he walked away.

League Table

	W	D	L	Pts	F	A	GD
All Saints	3	0	1	9	22	15	+7
Lawton	2	2	0	8	20	16	+4
Ridgeway	2	1	1	7	15	10	+5
Thornside	2	1	1	7	9	11	-2
Old Green	0	1	3	1	11	16	-5
Hawksmoor	0	1	3	1	8	17	-9

Top Goal Scorers

Jim Nasium (Lawton) 16
Jack Pott (All Saints) 13
Jaun Tu (Old Green) 10
David Jones (All Saints) 6
Markus Absent (Thornside) 5
Robin Banks (Ridgeway) 5
Leon Mee (Ridgeway) 4
Riley Thompson (Hawksmoor) 4
Ronny Thompson (Hawksmoor) 4

Daniel Williams (Lawton) 4
Ray Deo (All Saints) 3
Mike Raphone (Thornside) 2
Robert Smyth (Thornside) 2
Simon Kling (Ridgeway) 2
Owen Cash (Ridgeway) 2
Thomas Green (Ridgeway) 1
Bailey Scott (Ridgeway) 1

After school, Tommy and Harry walked home together as usual. They knew the streets like the backs of their hands. It was a relatively short journey, which was why they were allowed to walk home together. They neared the top of Caxton Street, ready to turn into Granville Street, to begin their routine race. Both boys would begin to walk a little bit quicker to ensure they had a great start, but would continue talking, pretending they weren't. In fact, this was the real beginning of the race. Harry was just ahead – as always – and turned the corner first, instantly launching into a sprint. Tommy turned into Granville Street next, immediately changing speed, looking up to see how far Harry was ahead so he could gauge how quickly he would need to run. To his surprise, though, Harry was nowhere to be seen and, more bizarrely, nor was Granville Street. Tommy slowed down to a walk, scanning the unfamiliar houses that now surrounded him. He spied a shop up on the corner and suddenly he knew exactly where he was. He approached the shop slowly, the big dusty sign above the window reading "Mr Ree's Sports Memorabilia". Tommy stood outside for a moment looking at the artefacts in the display area. There were old boots like the ones Mr Ree had given him, old photos, one of which Tommy now knew was Baz 'Smasher' McAllister, programmes, scarves, but it was the odd-looking keeper gloves that had really caught his eye. He climbed the steps and pushed the old wooden door open slowly. The small bell chimed at the back of the shop as the door creaked open. Tommy closed the door gently and saw the small old man in fawn-coloured overalls wearing the same strange-looking red hat that Tommy had to agree with Bailey looked more like a lampshade than an upside-down bucket.

'Hello, Tommy,' Mr Ree said casually.

Tommy approached the old counter. 'Hello,' he said.

'How are you finding the boots I gave you?'

'They are amazing, Mr Ree, thank you.'

'You've come to ask about the gloves in the window, haven't you?'

Well, I had just wanted to go home, Tommy thought. And what would Harry be thinking?

'You may borrow them if you like, but if you do, you will have to give me Stan's boots back, I'm afraid,' Mr Ree said matter-of-factly.

Tommy tried to weigh up what Mr Ree had just said. If the gloves were magic, they would definitely help Neil Downe, but what would Tommy do without the boots he had come to rely on? Mr Point had given him a letter for the match next Thursday, so what would he do if he had to play? On the other hand, if Lawton beat Thornside, it was all over anyway. How would he persuade Neil to wear them, though?

'Would you like to swap the boots for the gloves, Tommy?' Mr Ree pressed him.

'Okay,' Tommy sighed, hoping Bailey would be able to beat Hawksmoor.

He passed Stan's boots slowly over the counter. Mr Ree disappeared behind the thick purple curtain and reappeared with the old gloves. Tommy put them into his bag carefully.

'Right, Tommy, we had better be getting you home,' Mr Ree said. 'This way.'

Tommy followed him down the long corridor to his left. It seemed to go on forever; shelves stacked high from floor to ceiling. Eventually, they came to a door. It looked different from the one he'd gone through before.

Mr Ree opened it and stepped to one side. 'Here you go, Tommy, you should still have time,' he said with a wink and closed the door.

Time for what? Tommy wondered. He stepped out onto the corner of Caxton Street and Granville Street. He turned the corner and looked up to see Harry running for the third lamppost. Tommy broke into a sprint instinctively, trying to make sense of the last fifteen minutes and how no time seemed to have passed whilst he'd been in the shop. He caught Harry just before the third lamppost, exhausted.

'Close one,' Harry said cheerily. 'That gold will be mine soon, Tommy; I can feel it.'

'No chance,' Tommy grinned, trying to catch his breath.

'See you tomorrow, mate,' Harry called out as he walked the two doors up.

Tommy collected the key and let himself in. Shoes flicked off, fridge raided, TV remote in one hand and the strange old gloves that Mr Ree had given him in the other. Is this what Mr Ree had meant when he had told Tommy the shop would find him? He turned the gloves over in his hand. There was a name written near the stitching: C Ceseolli. They were bright orange and looked more like gardening gloves than goalie gloves. Convincing Neil to wear them was not going to be easy. Tommy put them on the settee and tucked into a sausage roll. He fast-forwarded to the Reds game that had been recorded the previous evening. The Reds captain came out of the tunnel to a rapturous applause and Tommy settled down to watch his heroes play, imagining what it would be like to be on the pitch with them.

CHAPTER 15

Jumpers for Goalposts

Tommy woke up early on Saturday morning. He pulled the special keeper gloves out from under his pillow and put them on. They felt comfortable enough, but they looked really old. To help persuade Neil to wear them against Lawton, Tommy had arranged a kick about down the park at 9am. He had invited Neil, Harry, Bailey, Chris, Artie, Leon, Ally and Wayne Dwops. Harry was bringing his World Cup ball and Bailey said she had some cones in her garage for the goals. The only thing he didn't have was boots! Now he'd given Stan's boots back to Mr Ree, he only had his school shoes. Oh well, they would have to do. He put his replica Reds kit on and stashed the gloves into a carrier bag. Next, he carefully placed Alf and Toni into his coat pocket and ran downstairs to eat his breakfast. Tommy was just starting his second slice of jam on toast when there was a knock at the door. He rushed to answer it, toast in his mouth.

'Hey, Tommy, are you ready?' Harry asked.

'Mmph,' Tommy replied through a mouthful of toast. 'Bye, Mum!'

'Ta-ra, pet,' she called back.

Neil was outside waiting in the street. The three boys made their way to the top of Granville Street and then made their way across to Ally's shop. Ally was outside waiting for them.

'All right?' he asked.

'All right, Ally?' they all chorused.

Next stop was Bailey's and then the park. Tommy rang

Bailey's doorbell and she appeared instantly, cones under her arm.

'Thought you'd forgotten me,' she said.

Never, thought Tommy, helping her with two of the cones. The park was at the top of the road. It had the usual slide, swings and climbing apparatus you see in most parks but was mainly used by the local cricket club. Cricket practice had begun ready for the new season, so the grass had been freshly cut. It looked like a snooker table, so flat and green. The sprinklers were on, watering the crease on an automatic arm that cascaded from side to side. It was still a bit cold to run through it, though.

The others were already there waiting for them, using a tennis ball for a quick game of Spot. Tommy made the two cones into a goal about four paces apart as Bailey did the same about fifty yards away. After a quick round of Ip Dip, Leon and Neil were named captains.

'Bailey,' Neil called out as his first pick. Tommy looked over jealously as Neil winked at Bailey.

'Ally,' replied Leon. *Bit predictable*, Tommy thought.

'Harry.' Tommy had not been expecting that, though! Did Neil really think Harry was better than him? Even worse, did Bailey?

'Tommy,' Leon called. *Oh, great, now I'm not on my mate's team*, Tommy thought.

'Artie.'

'Chris.'

'Wayne,' Neil concluded.

The two teams split up, Leon choosing ends because Neil had the first pick. Those who were wearing them piled their jumpers on top of one of the four cones, making the goals look like shaggy, multi-coloured mountain goats.

'Right, I'm up front, Ally's in goal and you two midfield and defence,' Leon ordered as he looked at Tom and Chris.

'Can I play in goal, Leon?' Tommy asked. 'I've brought my gloves.'

'What are those, your dad's gardening gloves?' Leon laughed back at him. 'No, Ally is a better keeper.'

'But they have five and we only have four!' Tommy argued. 'Can we play Rush Keeper?'

'That's a good idea,' said Ally. 'Besides, I'll get bored playing in goal all the time, I like to smash people,' he said with a smirk.

'Yeah, all right,' Leon conceded. 'We're playing Rush Keeper,' he shouted out to the other team.

'Yeah, all right,' Neil shouted back. 'You can start as you won't touch the ball much after kick off!' He laughed as he kicked Harry's ball at Leon.

Rush Keeper was a rule that allowed any player on your team to be the goalie, usually the nearest to the goal when the game was playing. This was perfect as Tommy could now try out the gloves in front of Neil.

Leon kicked off. Bailey had turned over possession quickly and started her attacking run. She only had Chris and Ally to beat as Leon and Tommy were behind her. Harry was just to her right, calling for the ball and giving Chris a difficult choice. He chose to try and tackle Bailey, who flicked the ball into Harry's path. Tommy ran straight towards the goal.

'Tackle him, Ally!' Tommy shouted. Ally didn't need telling twice, as he charged out towards Harry. Bailey had overlapped Harry and called for the ball to be played back to her. Harry passed the ball, but it hit Ally's knee and went high into the air. Tommy watched as he saw Bailey line up to volley the ball into the now empty net. His hands had begun buzzing like his feet as the magic started to do its thing. Tommy zoomed past Bailey but was facing the wrong way! How would he ever see the ball? Tommy heard the thump as Bailey's foot sweetly connected with Harry's ball. Tommy tried to turn his head, but his hands were pumping his arms so fast that he nearly punched himself in the face. Suddenly, his right arm shot straight up into the air with such force that Tommy was lifted off his feet like a superhero taking flight. He felt the ball striking the back of his hand and watched as the ball was deflected out for a corner.

Tommy landed on his hands, which softened his fall perfectly, and lay there smiling as he heard Leon shout out, 'Brilliant, Tommy!'

And Harry exclaimed, 'How did he do that?'

Bailey arrived by his side and offered him her hand. Tommy accepted the lift up, still smiling.

'Tommy, that was incredible!' She beamed at him and then ran over to take the corner, shaking her head in disbelief.

The group of friends played for the next two hours, and Tommy had yet to concede a single goal in the whole time. He had pulled off a string of saves that had been equally brilliant to the first.

'This is ridiculous!' called out Leon, who, after swapping teams at ten nil (he had scored eight of them), saw another excellent shot be calmly caught by Tommy as if it were the easiest thing in the world.

Bailey was as equally perplexed. 'Let's have a penalty shootout. First to score past Tommy gets an ice pole from Ally's shop on me.'

'Yeah, all right!' Tommy beamed confidently. *This will really impress Neil*, he thought.

Harry went first because it was his ball. He struck it well, bottom left, but Tommy's tingling fingers threw his right hand out and pushed the ball wide.

Leon was next. 'That ice pole's mine, Green,' he snarled. He took an extra-long run up and absolutely smashed the ball towards the top-right corner. Tommy's left hand just flung out and caught the ball like it was a balloon, then he stood there smiling with the ball under his arm.

'How?' Neil asked, puzzled. He'd been watching Tommy all morning and couldn't believe what he was seeing. Tommy hated playing in goal to the point where he would rather play matches without one if nobody wanted to go in. Something fishy was going on.

'It's these gloves, Neil, they're magic!' Tommy exclaimed.

'Magic, like fairy dust and that?' Leon teased, as some of them laughed at him. Even Harry and Bailey were trying not to smile.

'Honestly, I got them from this weird little shop with these cards. Tommy fished Alf and Toni out of his sock and held them out. 'Look.'

The little group huddled around.

'They're just old cards, Tommy, what are we supposed to be looking for?' Neil asked.

'They move and talk,' Tommy replied.

'Right, I've had enough of this rubbish, he's trying to make us look like idiots,' Leon huffed, throwing Alf back towards Tommy. 'I'm getting an ice pole anyway, anyone else coming?'

Wayne, Ally, Artie and Chris all followed him.

'Right, now they've gone, Tommy, tell us the truth, how did you get to be so good in goal?' Neil asked him.

'I'm telling the truth, Neil. Here, try them on and I'll take a penalty against you.' Tommy handed them to Neil.

The tall boy turned them over in his hands, studying them, and then threw them onto the floor at Tommy's feet. 'I thought we were mates, Tommy,' he said, then turned and walked away.

Tommy turned and looked at Harry and Bailey. 'You guys believe me, don't you?' he asked.

'We want to, Tommy,' Harry replied, 'but it does seem

a little – you know – far-fetched, mate.' Bailey shrugged in silent agreement.

'We spent ages looking for this shop the other month and it was nowhere to be seen, was it?'

'Just try them on, Harry. Bailey, you take the penalty, and you'll both see I'm telling the truth,' Tommy implored.

'All right, mate, giz 'em 'ere.' Harry stretched out his hand and took them off Tommy.

Bailey collected the ball and spotted it routinely. She took three steps backwards.

'Can you feel your fingers tingling?' Tommy asked.

'Er, no, but I think something is biting my thumb,' Harry retorted.

'That's the magic.' Tommy beamed.

'Spider, more like!' Bailey sniggered. 'Ready, Harry?'

'Yep.'

Bailey kicked the ball expertly into the bottom right corner as Harry dove the wrong way. Now it was Tommy's turn to look on in disbelief. Harry got up off the floor and collected his ball whilst Bailey picked up her cones.

'My lunch is probably ready anyway,' she said.

Harry handed the gloves back to Tommy. 'It was kinda funny, though, Tommy, I really thought for a minute I was going to be like this awesome keeper or something.'

Tommy just hung his head, looking at the two football cards who were motionless in his hands. Alf stood there with his fixed smile bolted on. Tears were starting to sting his eyes. Bailey walked over and joined them. 'I'm not making it up, guys, honest,' Tommy whispered. He looked at his friends' faces and could see they thought he was insane 'I'm not making it up!' Tommy shouted. Then he ran as fast as he could towards the park entrance and out of the gate, tears streaming down his face.

Bailey looked at Harry, who just raised his eyebrows and

puffed out a stream of air in a bemused sigh. 'Something is definitely a bit strange, though, Harry. Some of those saves Tommy made today were next to impossible. And do you remember I thought the card looked different that day in the library?'

'Yeah, I remember, and Tommy hates to play in goal usually,' Harry agreed.

CHAPTER 16
Fairy Tales

Tommy had run flat out until his lungs were bursting. He doubled over, trying to catch his breath, at the same time trying to wipe the tears from his eyes with his sleeve. He had Alf and Toni gripped tightly in his right hand.

'You alright, lad?' Alf asked.

Tommy just glared silently at the now-animated figure smiling back at him. He looked up and spotted a drain in the road. Tommy walked purposefully over to it and posted both cards through the grate. 'I hate you!' he shouted as he dropped them into the darkness. Next, he looked at the orange gloves and threw them into someone's garden. It was not a garden he recognised and, as the red mist he was currently under slowly unveiled the real Tommy, he started to realise he was unsure of where he was. He walked slowly at first, wary of his environment, but then started to quicken his pace as the panic began to embrace him. He paused at the top of the road, carefully studying the only two options available to him, left and right. Tommy spotted the mysterious memorabilia shop at the end of the right turn, so he turned left and ran in the opposite direction quickly. There was no way he was going back in Mr Ree's shop after today. He got to the top of the road, scanning for a familiar street, but was greeted with the same two options. At the top of the right turn was the strange little shop. Tommy turned around and looked behind him. To his disbelief, the little shop was still behind him as well. *Impossible!* Tommy thought to himself. He turned left again and ran as quickly as he could, fear washing all over him in a cold sweat. At the end of the road, he was greeted with the same two options again. Anger and frustration began to replace the fear, hot tears biting at his cheeks. Tommy clenched his fists as he strode quickly towards Mr Ree's shop, a false confidence driven by rage spurning him onwards. Tommy began to rehearse in his head what he was going to tell Mr Ree he could do with his little shop, which ordinarily would have been impossible, but now the gloves were quite literally off. As Tommy approached the old wooden door, he saw a handwritten notice stuck onto the window from the inside: Gone to lunch.

'Aaaaaarghhhh!' Tommy shouted out, exasperated. He slumped down on the steps, conscious that he was now also hungry, with no choice but to wait for Mr Ree to return, he supposed. Time always went so slowly when there was nothing to do, like sitting in class with Grumpy Grimshaw. Tommy glanced over his shoulder at the historical artefacts in the window. One of the programmes caught his eye. It was an old Reds programme from back in the day. They were playing their biggest rivals, the Blues. The date said 23rd of January 1937. *Wow*, thought Tommy. World War two started just over two years later, on the 1st of September 1939. He'd remembered that date from one of Grimshaw's lessons because she had made him write it out fifty times in his book. Tommy had mistakenly written the date off the board in his work instead.

'So, you think World War Two started today, do you, Mr Green?' Tommy could still hear the chorus of sniggers that had followed.

Tommy hoped the Reds had won. Next, he spotted an action figure with a blue strip on from the 1970s. He was way too big to get a place in Tommy's Magnificent Seven, and he was wearing blue, so that just wouldn't do. Just in front of him was a strange black disc that was apparently some sort of music. The label read: "Cup final anthem from 1973". It also said on the disc it was their cup. Although Tommy couldn't be completely sure, he thought he remembered his dad telling him that he went to see the Reds take "their" cup off them a year later in 1974. Tommy smiled at the thought of both his dad and the Reds winning the cup. *Where is Mr Ree?* Tommy thought. He'd been ages! Tommy turned and tried the door handle. To his surprise, it opened, and the bell above him rang. Mr Ree was sitting behind the counter cleaning something with a rag.

'Mr Ree, how long have you been back?' Tommy asked.

'Back from where, Tommy?'

'Lunch.'

'Lunch?'

'The sign on the door says you've gone to lunch.'

'Whoops, that was from yesterday,' Mr Ree laughed. 'Be a good lad and take it down for me.'

Tommy shook his head slowly from side to side. The sudden realisation he'd been sitting outside for nothing for the last half an hour sapped the last of his energy as he pulled the handwritten sign carefully off the glass. He walked over towards Mr Ree and put it on the counter.

'Mr Ree, why can't my friends use the magic gloves?' he asked.

'Simple, Tommy. Like I told you before: because they do not need them.' Mr Ree replied, not looking up from his cleaning. 'Have you brought them back?'

'Er, no,' Tommy spluttered, colour rising hotly in his cheeks. 'They're at home,' he lied.

'Well, be careful with them because they are only on loan and someone else may need them in the future,' Mr Ree explained. 'Although I was quite surprised you decided to take them, I thought you liked scoring goals more than saving them.'

'Yeah, I do, but they were for a friend.'

'Ah, I see. Unfortunately, Tommy, that's not how this all works, I'm afraid.'

'How does it all work then? Why is it only for me?' Tommy asked as his stomach growled.

Mr Ree put down his cleaning and pulled a chocolate bar out of his apron pocket. He slid it across the counter towards Tommy and then sat back, taking off his glasses and rubbing his nose. Tommy accepted the chocolate gratefully and took a big bite. 'You have heard of fairy godmothers, yes?' asked Mr Ree.

'Mmmphh,' Tommy nodded through a mouthful of chocolate.

'Guardian angels?'

Tommy nodded again.

'We have had many names over the years. Pixies, genies, sprites, wizards, witches, aliens, elves, devas, goblins, ghosts and my personal favourite: imaginary friends!' Mr Ree laughed. 'There have been many more, but as with all things, there are good and bad ones.'

'Are you a good one?' Tommy asked nervously.

Mr Ree smiled. 'Would a bad one give you your cards back?' He lifted the rag he'd been using and there beneath were Alf and Toni. They did not look particularly pleased to see him as Mr Ree handed them back over to Tommy.

'Sorry, guys,' Tommy whispered to them as he slipped them back into his sock carefully.

'We will appear to people in many different forms depending on who they are and why we are needed,' Mr Ree continued. 'For you, Tommy, I am a shopkeeper in the coolest shop you could ever have imagined. For others, I have been a white rabbit, a metal giant, a winged horse and even a talking mirror.' Mr Ree looked straight at Tommy. 'The trouble is, people have become blind to the magic that is all around them, it has become the "norm" I think they call it. A caterpillar turning into a beautiful butterfly, a mushroom appearing overnight, a fish that can walk, a tower that defies gravity, dinosaurs, a protective shield that literally surrounds the world in which you live!' Mr Ree slumped in his chair. 'Many years ago, people had a lot more respect for magic and now sadly many do not believe in it at all, much like your friends. They all saw you perform wonderful things today that should be considered impossible and yet they would rather believe it was a fluke or you've been hiding what a good goalkeeper you are, and at the mere mention of magic they mocked you.' Mr Ree looked under the counter and pulled out a large, old and dusty looking book. He thumbed through a few pages until he found the one he was looking for. 'Here, have a look at this, Tommy. Can you guess which one is me?' He turned the book around and pointed to a black and white photo that looked more brown than grey. In the photo there was a lion, a witch and an old-looking cupboard. Tommy shrugged and pointed at the witch.

'Don't be silly, lad, witches are girls! I'm the lion.' Mr Ree shook his head like it should have been obvious and that being a lion was a much more plausible answer. All this magic talk was beginning to make Tommy's head spin. 'If people just accepted that they do not need to know all the answers and took more time to just appreciate the wonders around them, the world would be a more magical place for sure. Sadly, most people want to stare at moving pictures of other people doing wonderful things, instead of doing them themselves.'

Tommy's stomach made another loud audible noise. 'I think I'd better be getting home for my lunch, Mr Ree,' said Tommy.

'Yes, I guess you're right.' Mr Ree put his glasses back on the end of his nose and picked up a thin silver whistle that was next to a cup and saucer on the counter. He blew into it, but it made absolutely no sound. He put the whistle down and began to drum his fingers on top of the counter. After a few seconds, the curtain behind Mr Ree moved, but Tommy couldn't see what had caused it to do so. Suddenly, a box that Tommy recognised was pushed up on top of the counter with what looked like little hands either side of it. He tried to peer over the top to see what was on the other side, but the curtain moved again and whatever it was, was gone. 'Thank you, Kevin,' Mr Ree called out after it. Tommy looked at Mr Ree quizzically. 'If people just accepted that they do not need to know all the answers and took more time to just appreciate the wonders around them, the world would be a more magical place,' Mr Ree repeated.

'So, what you mean is, instead of trying to find out how the magic works, I should just enjoy it.'

'Exactly, Tommy,' Mr Ree agreed as he pushed the box towards him.

Inside the box were Stan's old boots. 'But I have not brought the gloves back yet,' Tommy stammered.

'Do you mean these ones?' Mr Ree reached under the counter and placed the orange gloves next to the box.

'How did you…?'

Mr Ree held up his hand and cut him off. 'If people just accepted that they do not need to know all the answers, and took more time to just appreciate the wonders around them…'

'The world would be a more magical place,' Tommy finished.

Mr Ree just smiled. 'Come on, lad, this way.' Tommy had the strangest feeling of déjà vu as he tucked the shoe box under one arm and followed Mr Ree down one of the corridors of shelves. It bent to the left then to the right and then to the left again, just like before.

'Here we are,' Mr Ree said as they came to the door. He opened it and stepped to one side. Tommy said thank you and walked down the path in front of him. He turned around to look over his shoulder and the door he'd just walked through had been replaced with what was now a normal-looking front door. A curtain twitched in the window, followed by a loud tap as an old man stared back at him.

'Clear off!' he shouted, waving his clenched fist at him.

Tommy just laughed and ran through the gateway onto Granville Street. He was at the opposite end from the school, so had a lot further to walk. As he got closer to his house, he spotted Bailey and Harry standing by the third lamppost.

'Hey, Tommy, where did you go?' Harry asked. 'Bailey has bought us all an ice pole from Ally's shop.'

Tommy was about to tell them and then stopped himself. Instead, he just smiled knowingly and gratefully took the cola flavoured lolly from Bailey. 'Thanks,' he said.

'Are you okay, Tommy?' Bailey asked.

'Yeah, just hungry. See you guys at school.' Tommy turned and went inside his house. He shouted hello to his mum who was watching telly in the lounge and then headed straight to the fridge to raid whatever leftovers he could find. He sourced half a pork pie, three chunks of cheese, a jar of pickled onions and two chicken drumsticks. Next, he grabbed a packet of salt and vinegar crisps and a glass of orange squash. Balancing them all on a plate, he went up to his room. He began to write in his diary whilst shovelling food into his mouth with his left hand.

I went to Mr Rees' shop again today. He told me that he used to be a talking mirror and a lion! There is also something else in the shop called Kevin and it has these little hands.

He started to draw what he'd seen and then read back what he'd written. It sounded like something out of a fairy tale.

Tommy turned to look at Alf and Toni who were propped up on his pillow and in much better moods than earlier. Tommy read it out loud to them both. 'Should I tear the page out?' he asked them. 'It sounds crazy.'

'You're asking a talking player card, lad,' Alf replied.

'è tutto pazzesco,' Toni quipped.

'Aye, Toni is right, it is all a bit crazy when you stop and think about it.' Alf chuckled.

Tommy nodded and shoved two pickled onions, a chunk of cheese and three crisps into his mouth as he looked down at his drawing. *If people just accept that they do not need to know all the answers*, he thought to himself. He closed his diary and stashed it under the mattress. He took another pickled onion from the jar and pushed it into the half of pork pie then, in one go, shoved it all into his mouth, a contented look on his face as he lay back trying to chew it without choking. What was happening truly was magical and Mr Ree was right, he should just enjoy it, especially if he could get one over on Robin Banks.

CHAPTER 17

A Thorn in Your Side

It was Monday afternoon and Tommy was sitting in class, his mind on the Lawton versus Thornside match that was after school. Harry and Bailey were going to watch it with him as the result was so important. With Ridgeway and All Saints both playing on Wednesday as well, the league would be decided this week.

'Monsieur Green, pouvez-vous dire a la classe quel age as-tu?'

Oh no. Why always me?

'Guys, help me,' he whispered to his pencil case.

'Er, il ne parle pas francais,' Toni shouted out.

'C'est evident. Pourquoi un accent Italien?' replied Madame Parsons the French tutor, shaking her head.

'What did he say, Alf?' Tommy whispered.

'He told her you do not speak French,' Alf whispered back.

Oh, great, Tommy thought, but at least she was talking to someone else now. Tommy finished his lesson colouring a picture of a fish or "poisson", as it was called. Why anyone would want to call their food something that sounded like poison Tommy would never know. Can I have poison and chips twice please, pet, he imagined his mum ordering from the chippy. Yes, and curry sauce. They would need the curry sauce to help wash the poison down, Tommy thought, sniggering.

After school, he made his way with Harry up to the car park; Bailey was there waiting for them with her dad. Bailey's dad was not how Tommy imagined at all. He was quite short and stocky and had a neatly trimmed blonde beard and short hair.

'All right, boys,' he said as they approached.

'Hi, Mr Scott,' Tommy and Harry said in unison.

'Please call me Callum,' he said as he opened the back door of a swish, white sports car.

'Wow, this car is cool,' Harry cooed as he slid in.

Tommy joined him on the back seat. He had to admit it was neat. He particularly liked the red leather seats and imagined the Reds captain having something similar.

After a short hop across town, the three friends found a place to sit by the side of the Lawton pitch. Bailey's dad stood behind them.

'How come your dad is staying to watch, Bailey?' Tommy asked.

'He's scouting for players,' she replied matter-of-factly. 'I told him about Diego, and he wanted to see for himself.'

'What do you mean?' Harry asked, suddenly interested.

'Well, he used to coach my team in my old town and seeing as Bowden Park wouldn't let me try out, he decided he would make his own team.'

'Cool,' Tommy and Harry chorused as Tommy started to study Bailey's dad more carefully.

'Did your dad play at all, Bailey?' Tommy asked.

'Yeah, he was signed by the Blues when he was ten but broke his leg at seventeen. Unfortunately, he never quite got back to academy standard. He was released a year later and played a bit of semi-pro stuff, but he got into coaching and retired from playing,' she explained.

'How come you never said before?' Tommy asked.

'You never asked, plus I know you don't like the blues,' she replied, laughing. 'And his head gets big enough when he name drops all the players he's played with or against.'

Tommy was slightly awestruck. He had so many questions

racing around in his head but was snapped back to attention when he heard a familiar voice.

'Hey, Bailey, you came to watch me then?' Neil Downe asked.

'No, she came to watch Diego,' Tommy interjected before Bailey could answer. 'Ow!' he gasped. 'Why did you hit me?'

Bailey didn't answer. Instead, she turned towards the centre circle as the Lawton teacher blew her whistle. Both sides looked ready for war. Jimbo shook hands with Markus Absent the Thornside skipper and then won the coin toss. A Lawton centre. Diego was starting today, which Tommy was not surprised about. Their team consisted of Jimbo as striker, a midfield three of Diego, Armand Oleg and Luke Warm, and a defensive pairing of Danny 'Tank' Williams and Stan Dup. Hans Tyd, minus a tooth, was back in goal.

Thornside lined up with Anna Konda upfront, Markus Absent centre midfield, Robert Smyth and Mike Raphone on the wings and Orson Kart and Rai Singh in defence. Neil 'flagpole' Downe was obviously in goal. Both sides had strengths and weaknesses, but would Diego be the deciding factor that just gave Lawton the edge?

Jimbo passed the ball back to Diego, who attacked straight away. Anna was the first to try and intercept him, but Diego just rolled the ball through her legs and advanced. Next, Smyth tried to slide tackle him, but Diego just lifted the ball over Smyth's legs and hurdled the human barrier. Markus managed to steal the loose ball, though, and played it back to Singh. Jimbo put him under pressure quickly, forcing Singh to play back to Neil, who launched a big kick straight up the field. The ball sailed high and long. Tommy looked on in earnest as the ball continued to soar.

'It's going in!' Harry exclaimed excitedly, pulling at Tommy's sleeve.

The Three Amigos watched in a trance as the ball fell

from the sky over the flailing arms of Hans 'mind the gap' Tyd who had been far too far off his line.

'Get in!' Tommy called out.

'Good shot, Neil!' Bailey shouted towards the now moon-walking goalkeeper. Downe finished his move with a spin and then the splits just as Markus Absent arrived late to high five him. Unbelievably, Downe was almost as tall as Markus was when sitting on the ground.

One-nil to Thornside.

Jimbo took the kick-off again, this time passing straight back to Tank. Tank tried to emulate Downe with a long shot but, at nearly a foot taller than Hans, Neil just caught the ball comfortably. He rolled it out to Singh, who passed down the line to Kart. Orson Kart was not a bad player and was confident enough to attack Stan Dup. Trouble was, Stan hardly ever got to kick the ball as Danny Williams just marshalled the defence on his own. Kart galloped past him easily, only to be hit by Tank. Jimbo yelled for a long pass as he circled the edge of the Thornside penalty area and Williams obliged with a perfectly chipped pass straight to Jimbo's feet. Raphone closed him down quickly, giving him no space to turn, but Jimbo had no intention of shooting. Instead, he passed the ball short to Diego, who ran through on goal. Singh tried to tackle him, but Diego dropped his shoulder and sent him the wrong way. Downe was screening across to try and block any possible shot, but Diego kept going, getting closer and closer. Neil rushed towards him, diving at his feet, but this was just what Diego wanted. He'd drawn Neil into committing himself and now coolly back-heeled the ball into the path of the expectant Nasium. Kart tried in vain to get to the ball first, but to no avail, and Jimbo toe-poked the ball home.

All square again at one-all.

'Argh!' said Tommy. 'How did Neil fall for that?'

'It wasn't really his fault, Tom. Orson should have passed quicker,' Harry argued.

'Don't be so quick to blame the keeper, Tommy,' Bailey concurred.

Markus Absent took the centre with Anna, and play resumed. Downe was not moving from goal now, refusing to be duped again. Thornside had switched to a back three of Singh, Kart and Lee King who had been subbed in for Smyth. King had played in goal for Downe in the game against Ridgeway.

'Let's hope Lee does better on pitch than he did in goal, Tommy,' Harry remarked.

Tommy just nodded, still sore that Bailey had defended Downe. *She must really fancy him,* Tommy thought to himself glumly. Thornside were being blitzed by Diego, Jimbo and Tank. Markus Absent had hardly got out of his half; instead, he just sat in front of the defence, trying to force shots from a distance. Lawton knew a draw would not be enough to win the league and were in all-out attack mode against a very resilient defence.

Tommy started to think about the Roman tortoise or "testudo", as they called it. It was a formation used by Roman soldiers with their shields to approach enemy fortifications. The soldiers would march up to a fort in the testudo formation with their shields fitting so closely together that they formed one large shield. It looked a bit like a giant tortoise shell. Arrows and spears could not get through the gaps to hurt the soldiers beneath and so they could approach the gates unharmed. This was about the only thing Tommy had found interesting about the Romans because his grandad owned a tortoise called Brian that he kept in his shed. Tommy had tried to make Brian walk into a pretend fort he'd made out of empty flowerpots. Tommy had crouched down behind the fort with an empty bucket on his head and a pile of picked dandelion heads in his hand. He'd then thrown the "dandelion bombs" at Brian, but instead of charging into the flowerpot fort, Brian had simply stopped and happily munched on most of Tommy's ammo supply.

'Goal!'

Tommy snapped back from his daydream just in time to see Diego wheeling away with his arms in the air.

'Wow, did you see that, Tom?' Harry said, nudging his mate in the arm.

'Neil was unlucky, though, Harry, he saved the first shot,' Bailey defended him again.

'Yeah, but that bicycle kick was sick, wasn't it, Tommy?'

'Er, yeah,' Tommy lied, having completely missed it whilst thinking about Brian the tortoise.

Two-one: Lawton.

With the lead now in place, Lawton had slowed their barrage, happy to protect the lead. They still went close a couple of times before halftime, though, with Jimbo hitting the post and Downe making a great save from a Tank buster special. Lawton had made two changes with Cliff Anga coming on for Hans Tyd and Danny Williams had gone in goal. The Lawton coach had switched to a three-two-one formation and had told Oleg to play up front as a lone striker. Jimbo and Diego were now playing central midfield together with Dup, Anga and Warm in defence.

'Lawton have switched to a testudo,' Tommy said out loud.

'A what, Tom?' Harry asked.

'Never mind,' he replied.

'It's called a low block in football, Tommy,' a voice behind him said.

Tommy looked up to see Bailey's dad with a notebook in his hand. He was scribbling something down. 'When a team sits deep and plays a low block, they are trying to deny space

149

in behind. It is a very defensive move, also known as parking the bus.'

Bailey rolled her eyes. 'See, he goes on a bit,' she whispered to both the boys, smiling.

'You were right as well, Bailey; that Diego lad is a good player. I will need to find his parents afterwards and see if they are interested in him joining our team,' Mr Scott said without looking up from his writing.

Tommy would've loved to have seen what he was writing. He didn't think Mr Scott was going on at all and would have loved to sit and chat to him for hours. Bailey was so lucky. Tommy started to think about his dad and the times they had sat watching the football roundup together. His dad would pause the TV and analyse the game for Tommy before the pundits had their chance to speak.

'There you go, Tommy, what did I say?' he would proudly announce as the pundits almost repeated word for word what he'd said ten minutes earlier.

'Oh, no!' Harry called out.

Tommy looked up just in time to see Jimbo tapping the ball into an empty net and Neil Downe punching the floor.

Three-one to Lawton.

'Well, that's it!' Harry declared. 'Thornside are done for.'

'There's still ten minutes to go, Harry,' Bailey said encouragingly, but Tommy wasn't convinced she believed it.

The Thornside coach was calling over Markus. After a few brief words and some stern looks from the ref, Absent kicked off. Lawton were happy for Thornside to have the ball in their half, knowing that they'd done enough and just needed to see the game out. Armand Oleg was the only one pressing and the Thornside players began a game of piggy in the middle with him. Lee King ran into the Lawton area and stood face to face with Danny Williams, although it was more face to chest as Williams towered over him. Every time

Williams moved, Lee mirrored him. Tommy could see this was beginning to irritate Williams, who now also had Stan Dup next to him as Dup tried to mark Lee. Next, Konda went and stood in front of Williams and started mirroring both King and Tank. Seeing this, Cliff Anga went to track Anna, so now there was a strange tribal dance going on in the six-yard box. The ref looked over but, as no rules were being broken, she turned her attention back to the ball. Absent was in possession on the edge of his area, teasing Oleg, who was very red-faced and slightly out of breath. Nasium and Diego watched, poised on the halfway like sentry guards. Absent shouted instructions to Raphone and Singh to push up, which they did, taking a wing each. This meant that Thornside had now overloaded the Lawton defence four players to three with Stan Dup now unsure which of the wide players to mark. Diego saw what was happening and tracked Singh, leaving just Jimbo on the halfway line. Oleg lunged in on Markus, who calmly played the ball back to Neil Downe. With Oleg on the floor, Downe dribbled out of his box as Absent and Kart both ran straight at Jimbo. Just before they crossed the halfway line, they split and ran in opposite directions. Jimbo was now in a one-on-one against Downe. The temptation of a hat trick was just too strong and he ran out of his half to close Downe down. Neil was not daft enough to try and take Jimbo on. Instead, he coolly chipped the ball over him, where Markus collected it brilliantly on his thigh. Thornside now had a six versus four in an overload. Diego turned and ran to intercept, whilst Jimbo gave chase from behind. Markus ran to the right-wing, drawing Diego and Jimbo away from the goal. Just as Diego arrived, Markus transferred the ball to the other wing where Mike Raphone was waiting. Stan Dup was like a rabbit in headlights as Raphone dribbled towards him. Kart made an overlapping run on the outside, creating a four versus two overload in Thornside's favour. With the Tank in goal, Stan Dup had no idea what to do and, instead, fell over as Raphone buzzed past him. Williams rushed out and tried to slide tackle Raphone rather than use his hands, his defender instincts taking over. Mike merely passed the ball to his right where Kart was waiting to shoot.

Three-two, Lawton.

Jimbo was still going nuts at Stan as he spotted the ball for centre. Tank was blaming Anga and Dup and Diego was saying something in Portuguese – mainly with his hands – to Williams. Tommy wasn't sure what he was saying, but Williams did not look too happy about it. Lawton were not so confident now, with every pass looking nervous. The momentum had shifted and Thornside pressed hard, chasing every pass. Only Diego seemed confident on the ball still. As players ran at him, he would just either sidestep them, or dribble away from them, shielding the ball as he did so. Not once did he enter the Thornside half, though, determined to just wind the clock down by keeping possession. Lee King was back in the Lawton box trying to annoy Tank Williams. Hans Tyd was back on for Oleg, who had requested a sit down, and had been given the task of standing between King and Williams. Hans was refusing to be drawn into a dance off with King, instead just blocking him from getting to Tank. Lawton were no longer playing with a striker. The coach had chosen to go with two banks of three, as he tried to hold onto the slender one goal lead. Thornside, on the other hand, were much more attacking. With no striker to worry about, Neil Downe was outside his box playing as sweeper. This allowed Thornside to play much higher and press into the Lawton half.

Lawton had stayed disciplined for a good five minutes, but Jimbo had clearly been eyeing up the goal that Downe had left unattended as the idea of a hat trick ate away at him. He knew he could score from the halfway line, he'd done it many times; just one more goal and that would be it, game over, plus he'd be the hat trick hero in assembly. He drifted out wide and called Diego for the ball. Diego, in the midst of teasing Singh, flicked the ball with the outside of his boot straight to Jimbo's left foot. Jimbo smashed the ball first time high into the air as he tried to lob Downe. It nearly worked too, but Downe had been expecting someone to try it and backpedalled quickly enough to get both hands onto the ball. Turnover of possession. Thornside could now attack. Downe threw the ball to the floor and dribbled forwards. With nobody in his half to stop him and the pitch so small, he was on the halfway line in seconds and shot for goal. Jimbo had realised his error and ran back to defend the goal rather than fall for being drawn out of position again. Diego had done the same and was back in time to block the shot with his head. The ball arched high into the air and Tank ran out to catch it. With his eyes on the ball, he'd forgotten about Lee King, who stepped in front of him. Tank crashed into him and went sprawling, knocking into Hans as well. The ball dropped just out of Tank's reach, landing in front of Stan Dup instead. Stan panicked and tried to just kick it away, but Absent blocked the clearance and the ball ricocheted into the path of Mike Raphone. Raphone shot for the empty goal, but Jimbo, who had kept running back, slid in to put the ball wide for a corner. After being run over by a tank, Lee King was subbed off for Rick O'Shea

The Three Amigos sat silently, knuckles white, hearts almost stopped, eyes transfixed on Markus Absent who had the ball at the corner flag.

'Rai, you take it, you take it,' he called, holding the ball out in his hands. Singh, who was not expecting this, dutifully ran over to his captain. Just as Singh approached, Absent slammed the ball to the floor and kicked the ball straight at his feet. Singh stopped the ball with the sole of his foot just

153

as Absent arrived to take it back off him. Jimbo rushed from his near post position to block any shots, but Markus just scooped the ball towards the back post instead. Diego was waiting and lined himself up to control the ball on his chest, but he did not get the chance. Neil Downe jumped high up in front of him and headed the ball towards the goal. Downe had waited until everyone had taken their positions and then quietly made his way to the opposite corner flag where no one was watching. Once Absent had taken the corner, Neil had run quickly, unmarked, in on the back post and beat Diego easily in the air with his superior height advantage. Diego was brilliant with the ball at his feet, but he couldn't be brilliant if he couldn't reach it. Danny Williams was quick, though, and used his large frame to block the header with his knee. The ball rebounded straight into an unmarked Rick O'Shea, who deflected the ball into the goal with his face.

Three-all.

There was a short delay as Rick was taken off with a slight concussion and the hugest grin they had ever seen. Jimbo and Diego were both at the centre, poised for the whistle. There could only be seconds left until full time and now Lawton had to score again.

Jimbo passed to Diego who was off in a flash. He snaked around Anna Konda, then megged Kart, flip-flapped past Singh, six stepovers later and Raphone was on his backside. Markus tried to slide him but Diego turned him and was through on goal. Smyth now back on for Rick was too far away to stop him shooting as Diego curled the ball with the outside of his left boot, aiming at the far top corner of the net. It was a great shot and not many people would have stopped it, but Neil Downe timed his leap perfectly and got one of his long arms across, tipping the ball out for a corner with his fingertips.

Full time.

Tommy blew out his cheeks with a sigh of relief as he glanced over at Harry, whose grin covered his whole face.

'Game on, then,' Bailey said as she hauled the two lads to their feet.

Bailey's dad dropped the boys off at the third lamppost. Tommy and Harry had been chatting about Diego all the way back. Neither could understand why Robin Banks had been scouted for United and Diego wasn't even in a local team yet.

'Maybe if he does play for Bailey's dad he will get scouted soon,' Harry reasoned.

'Yeah, maybe. I wonder if he would let us try out, Harry?' Tommy pondered.

'Let's ask Bailey at school tomorrow,' Harry said. 'It would be cool if we could all play together.'

'Good idea, see you later, Harry.'

Harry waved and ran on up to his house as Tommy fished his key out from under the mat. With tonight's draw, Ridgeway still had an outside chance of winning the league. Tommy opened the door and went inside to tell his diary all about it.

CHAPTER 18

Spy Games

At School, Tommy was looking at the team sheet for Wednesday with Bailey. With no Owen Cash and no Banks and Edward Long's mum declaring football was too rough for him, Tommy and Harry were both in the squad.

Liam Mackenzie
GK

Ally Gayter   *Harry Smith*
CB   *CB*

Simon Kling   *Bailey Scott*   *Tommy Green*
RW   *CM*   *LW*

Leon Mee
ST

Subs:
Terry Bull
Wayne Dwops
Rohan De Boat
Justin Case

'Terry Bull is back in the team,' Bailey said surprised. 'Look, Mr P has also added an extra sub, Justin Case.'

'Let's hope Terry gets his laces done up properly this time,' Tommy quipped.

'Well, at least Mr P is starting you and Harry this time. I bet Rohan's not happy, though.'

Just as she spoke, De Boat, Banks and Owen Cash came round the corner. Cash was still on crutches with his ankle strapped up.

'Hope you're happy now, Green? You and your mate Smithy have wormed your way into the team and now a quality player like Rohan here is being dropped. Mr Point has clearly lost it. Still, it won't matter if you do win. Jack Pott will roll Jaun Tu over into next week on Wednesday and you will still be a loser,' Banks sneered.

The three boys walked into their classroom, leaving Bailey and Tommy to look at the board.

'As much as I hate to say it, he's right. We should beat Hawksmoor, Tommy, but All Saints should also beat Old Green comfortably,' Bailey observed.

'It's just between us and All Saints now, Bailey, and it could go to goal difference as well, but we are two behind them. Hawksmoor have conceded a lot, but they have scored two goals in every game so far. The Thompson Twins have one a piece in every game. If they were to both score again, we'd need at least five goals to overtake All Saints, but that only matters if Old Green can earn a draw out of the game,' Tommy said as he studied the league table.

'Yeah, and Lawton were so unlucky last night. They score loads of goals, but without a great keeper they also let a lot in. That eight-seven game with All Saints was epic, though.'

'Looks like Jimbo beat his goal record from last year as well, eighteen is amazing,' Tommy pointed out.

'Yeah, but look at their pitch, Tommy. The goals are so close together, it's no wonder they have such high scoring games.'

League Table

	W	D	L	Pts	F	A	GD
All Saints	3	0	1	9	22	15	+7
Lawton	2	3	0	9	23	19	+4
Thornside	2	2	1	8	12	14	-2
Ridgeway	2	1	1	7	15	10	+5
Old Green	0	1	3	1	11	16	-5
Hawksmoor	0	1	3	1	8	17	-9

Top Goal Scorers

Jim Nasium (Lawton) 18

Jack Pott (All Saints) 13

Jaun Tu (Old Green) 10

David Jones (All Saints) 6

Markus Absent (Thornside) 5

Robin Banks (Ridgeway) 5

Leon Mee (Ridgeway) 4

Riley Thompson (Hawksmoor) 4

Ronny Thompson (Hawksmoor) 4

Daniel Williams (Lawton) 4

Ray Deo (All Saints) 3

Mike Raphone (Thornside) 2

Robert Smyth (Thornside) 2

Simon Kling (Ridgeway) 2

Owen Cash (Ridgeway) 2

Thomas Green (Ridgeway) 1

Bailey Scott (Ridgeway) 1

Diego Ortiz (Lawton) 1

Orson Kart (Thornside) 1

Rick O'Shea (Thornside) 1

Neil Downe (Thornside) 1

'Bailey, do you think your dad would let us try out for his team?' Tommy blurted out suddenly. He'd been waiting for a good opportunity to ask but impatience had got the better of him and he was desperate to know.

'I thought you'd never ask!' Bailey laughed. 'And yes,

Harry can come too. My dad had already asked me to invite you both along.'

Tommy was still smiling as he sat in his art lesson painting a vase with some flowers in. Tommy liked art and was enjoying trying to mix the right shade of yellow with his watercolours. Mr Meener was supposed to be marking books at the front of the class but he had clearly fallen asleep. No one was in a rush to wake him, and some people were now just chatting or eating leftover snacks from their lunchboxes. Tommy was thinking about Wednesday. With both the games being played at the same time, it would be impossible to know if they'd won the league until Mr Point had been given the scores the next day. Tommy wasn't sure he could wait that long and so began to hatch a plan.

Tommy had told Harry and Bailey that he was meeting his mum in town, but really, he was on his way to Old Green Primary School. It was not that far from Ridgeway and soon Tommy was outside the main gates. Most of the parents had been and collected their children and gone home; just the odd one or two were still milling around nattering to each other. Tommy checked that no one was looking and climbed over the wooden perimeter fence. He'd been to Old Green a few times and knew exactly what he was looking for. It was a large oak tree that the school was named after. Old Green was over two hundred years old and stood pride of place in the middle of the school field, giving the children plenty of shade in the summer. It was also very close to the school football pitch and that's why Tommy needed it now. He darted across the open space and hid on the opposite side of the tree, away from the school windows. He counted to twenty and then peered around the side of the giant tree's trunk to check no one was coming. The coast was clear. Tommy pulled the magic cards out of his pocket and addressed them.

'Right are you sure this will work?' Tommy asked.

'Si, si, Tommy, az long as it Noah rain, no?' Toni replied.

'It will be fine, lad, no one will think to look up a tree for Toni's card,' said Alf.

'Okay,' Tommy said a little hesitantly. He didn't like this part of the plan, but he could see no other way as he couldn't be in two places at once. He shimmied up the tree and sat on the lowest branch. It had a great view of the pitch, which was perfect for his plan. Using a drawing pin he'd acquired from the sleeping Mr Meener's desk, Tommy affixed Toni's card to the branch so he was facing the pitch, then climbed back down. He held Alf's card in his hand and waited. Sure enough, a few seconds later, a beaming Toni appeared. Okay, so far so good. The next day, Alf would be able to pop back and forth from the action and let Tommy know the Old Green score. Tommy checked the coast was clear and made his way back the way he'd come. He hopped back over the fence and ran home as quickly as he could.

After his tea, Tommy fished out his diary and began to write.

I hate Robin Banks. I really hope we win the league tomorrow without him playing. I can't wait to play tomorrow but I am worried that I won't play well and end up losing us the game.

Tommy closed his diary and stashed it under his mattress, said goodnight to Alf and Toni and switched off his lamp. He closed his eyes tight and wished for the next day to come quickly.

At school, there was a buzz in the corridors, everyone talking about the game. Emma was chatting to her friends by the girls' toilets.

'No, I had to dump Rohan. I can't go out with a substitute. Anyway, Si has a nicer bike,' she was saying loudly.

Tommy ignored them and walked past with his head down, looking to find Bailey and Harry. They were waiting for him by the sports board.

'Hey!' Tommy called out as he approached them.

'Hey, Tommy,' they both chorused in reply.

'Have you remembered your boots, mate?' Harry asked, smirking.

'Yes, I've got my boots.' Tommy mock sighed, holding up his laden carrier bag.

Suddenly, the bag was snatched from Tommy's outstretched hand. Banks!

'Oi, give 'em back, Banksy,' Tommy demanded.

'Come and get them, squirt,' Banks teased as he held the bag up high.

Tommy jumped up, trying to snatch the bag back, but Banks kept pulling it out of his reach.

'Give them back, Robin,' Bailey echoed.

'Ah, your little girlfriend is fighting your battles for you, so sweet,' Banks mocked. 'Here, Rohan, catch!' Banks said as he threw the bag through the air.

De Boat caught Tommy's bag and pulled out one of Stan's boots. 'These things are well manky,' he said, holding one up by the laces. 'And they stink!' he said, pulling a face.

'That's 'cause Green's been wearing them,' Banks laughed.

Rohan threw the boot over to Si Kling, who volleyed it towards the bin. It hit the rim and skidded off around the corner.

'Ooh, unlucky, Si,' Banks sniggered.

Harry ran off around the corner after it as De Boat threw

the other boot back over to Banksy.

'Urrgh, no thanks,' he called out, stepping to one side.

'Ow!' The boot had hit Terry Bull on the head. A large gash appeared. Terry put his hand instinctively to where the boot had hit him and nearly fainted as he inspected the wet substance in his hand.

Banks laughed out loud. 'Come on, boys, we'd better get to class,' he said.

Tommy retrieved his boot from the floor just as Harry returned with the other one.

'I'm taking Terry to Mrs Flett. He does not look well,' Bailey said over her shoulder as she led him away.

Tommy put his boots back in the carrier bag and he and Harry shuffled off to Mr Meener's next lesson.

'So, five times nine is?' Mr Meener hung the question in the air.

'Forty-five,' the class chorused.

Mr Meener wrote the equation on the whiteboard under the ten times nine that he'd previously written. 'What do you notice?' he asked.

Tianna Bizkit's hand shot up. 'Because five is half of ten, the answer is also half.' She beamed.

'Well done, Tianna, have a House point. Tommy,' he said. 'Using the answers on the board, can you tell me what six times nine is?'

Tommy hated maths but he understood how to add nine to numbers because nine points was three wins. His dad had shown him how to work out league tables when he was in year one. It was also how Tommy had learnt to read. Recognising team names at first and then starting to read the reports with his dad in the paper.

'Fifty-four,' he called out confidently.

'Yes, well done, Tommy, you can have a House point too.'

Tommy caught Harry's eye and gave him a cheeky wink. Only forty more House points to go and he could have a certificate. Harry was on his third certificate already!

Riiiinnng.

'Out to break, all of you, file out sensibly, please.'

As if! The class filed out as usual, pushing and shoving each other left and right, but Tommy was first through, ducking under Tianna's arm as she struggled to stay upright. He ran/fast-walked around the winding corridors and out into the fresh air. He waited for Harry and the others at the top playground as the usual junior class spectators started to gather, munching on a variety of chocolate bars and packets of crisps. Mr Binrite had tried to make the school "healthy" and had banned all snacks, insisting the pupils could only eat fruit, but this had started an underground snack smuggling ring run by GO6L. If you paid them 50p, they would sneak you a chocolate digestive and stand watch outside the toilets whilst you scoffed it in the cubicles. When the PTA discovered what was happening, they had forced Mr Binrite to reinstate all snacks by threatening to boycott the Easter bingo. Tommy looked at the white rectangle on the wall of the pavilion. He studied the little bits of flaky paint that had come loose where the ball had struck it. He was surprised how bare the top bins were considering how many times they'd lost. Harry arrived and placed his ball on the centre circle. It was now difficult to tell it was a replica World Cup ball as most of the markings had worn off from all the games they'd played on the hard concrete floor.

The GO6L lads arrived but these days they walked in two separate groups. Mac's group walked over to where Tommy and Harry were standing, and Banks and the others walked towards the pavilion goal.

'All right, lads?' Mac asked.

'Yeah, you?' Tommy replied.

'I will be better after we batter Banksy.' He smiled as he made his way to the fence goal, high-fiving Bailey as she ran over to join them.

'Hey,' she said, slightly out of breath. 'Terry Bull has gone to hospital to have stitches, so he's out of the lineup tonight.'

'That sucks for him,' Harry said.

'Has Mr P drafted anyone in to replace him?' Tommy asked.

'Not that I can tell,' Bailey replied.

'Come on, Green, wasting time won't help you stop getting whipped again!' Banks shouted over.

Tommy stood over the ball and kicked it backwards to Gayter. Ally passed to Leon, who started to run at Si Kling. Kling had anticipated this and clattered into him hard, both boys collapsing in a heap. The ball popped loose, and Bailey pounced on it, trapping it expertly under her foot. De Boat swung a leg at the ball, but Bailey just scooped it up over his foot and waltzed past him. Banks was next, as he rushed in with every intent of hurting her, but Bailey had seen him and flicked the ball out to Tommy. Banks tried to prevent the pass but failed. Tommy played the ball on his first touch towards the pavilion as he skirted the edge of the playground. He was clean through. He pulled his leg back and aimed to the left of Artie Choak, who Banks had made go in goal, but as he swung his leg, Owen Cash tripped him with one of his crutches, sending him tumbling to the floor. Banks nicked the ball and chipped it over Bailey, straight into Kling's path. Harry rushed out to block him, but Kling rolled the ball to his right and Rohan smashed the ball through Mac's legs.

One-nil.

Since Mac and Banks had fallen out, the two teams were more balanced. Banks, having lost a number of his class, had coerced Chris, Wayne and Artie to play for him. Chris and Artie were helping Tommy to his feet in front of the sniggering Cash.

'What are you two doing?' Banks screamed at them. 'He's on the other team, leave him alone or else.'

'Sorry, Tommy,' Chris whispered.

Bailey spotted the ball on the centre circle. 'You okay, Tommy?' she asked.

Tommy nodded. Bailey took three steps back and shaped up like she was going to shoot.

'Watch out, she's shooting!' Kling called across to his team. Instinctively Banks and the others moved backwards to cover the goal. Bailey took a deep breath and ran at the ball, but instead of shooting, she turned at the last minute and aimed straight into the crowd.

'Owwww!' came a shrill noise from in the pack. 'My node!' The ball had struck Owen Cash straight in the face and lifted him off his crutches and onto his backside.

Tommy's team, including Tommy, burst into laughter as the crowd parted, revealing the stranded Cash who was sitting clutching his face.

The game had finished a two-all draw with Bailey scoring two and Banks scoring their second. Tommy and Harry were now doing "quiet reading", which Tommy was convinced was just to give Mr Meener a break rather than having any real benefit for the class. Tommy had a big atlas standing open on his desk, which allowed him to read his comic without being seen. Harry was doing the same but was using a large children's encyclopaedia.

'Sir, Tommy's reading a comic,' came a voice from behind him.

Tommy span round to see Isabel Ringer with her hand up. Tommy turned back around just as Mr Meener arrived at his desk. He lifted the atlas up and looked at Tommy's comic.

'Oh dear, Tommy, and you had such a good morning,' Mr Meener said, actually sounding disappointed. Tommy slumped in his chair as he realised he'd just lost his lunchtime again. He glanced over at Harry, who was slowly sliding his comic up his jumper.

Tommy had sat outside Mr Binrite's room during lunchtime, ironically reading his comic. In the afternoon, he had double PE. Tommy loved PE most of the time, but he'd not enjoyed it this time. Mr Meener had made them play bench ball all afternoon. Being Tommy's size meant he had hardly touched the ball all afternoon. Even when it was his turn to be on the bench, he was still smaller than most of the class. Harry, on the other hand, had been in his element, scoring goals for fun. Now they were both sitting on Mr Point's classroom floor next to a red pitch marker watching Mr Point draw frantically on his whiteboard. Tommy glanced over at Rohan, Justin and Wayne, who were sitting on the chairs by the wall and the extra empty chair that should have been Terry's.

'Now, Simon, when Liam has the ball, I want you to drop in here but stay wide so that he can throw the ball to you and then...'

Cough. 'Excuse me, sir.' Everyone turned towards the classroom door. There in the doorway stood Robin Banks in full kit except for his shirt, which Tommy was wearing. 'If you need me to play, my dad says it's okay, but just this once.'

'That's wonderful news, Robin. Quickly, Tommy, give Robin his shirt and sit over there,' he said, pointing at the empty chair.

Tommy's heart sank as he pulled the shirt off and over his head. Banks snatched it from his grasp and pulled a face as he pretended to smell it. Tommy sat in his vest and shorts next to De Boat, who was grinning broadly. He watched as Banks sat down where he had been sitting just seconds earlier. Bailey and Harry both turned and looked at him, pity in their eyes. Tommy just looked down at his feet.

'Right, right, Simon ignore that, Robin will do it, won't you, lad?'

'Yes, sir,' Banks snapped back military style.

'Now Robin is here, he will take all the free kicks, corners and penalties as well.' Mr Point put the top on his pen and handed Banks the CD player.

'Sir, have you got a top for Tommy?' Bailey asked.

'No, unfortunately not, it's in my car and we don't have time to get it now. You'll be all right, won't you, Tommy lad?'

Tommy looked up forlornly and nodded, slipping his school jumper over his head.

'Good, well that's settled then. Robin, if you would be so kind.'

Banks stood and hit play on the CD player, and everyone filed in behind him and followed him out of the door. Tommy trudging along at the back.

'Tommy!' Tommy turned to see Mr Nomos with a broom in his hand. 'Remember what I always say to you, pass and move, pass and move. The best teams always pass and move.'

'I'm not even playing, Mr Nomos.' Tommy sighed.

'You will play, Tommy, I'm sure of it. Just be ready when you get your chance and…'

'Pass and move.'

'Exactamente.' Mr Nomos smiled.

Tommy caught up with the others. The Brazilian Beach Soccer Specials with custom red-and-black-striped nets were up and ready. Mr Nomos had outdone himself, as the pitch looked like a snooker table. Hawksmoor were already there warming up in their traditional navy and silver strip. Two tall ball boys were standing away from the main group. The Thompson twins, Riley and Ronny. They were standing facing each other approximately twenty-five yards away from each other just pinging the ball back and forth as hard as they could, expertly trapping the ball on one touch and then passing back on their second. Mr Point blew his whistle and Banks shook hands with both twins, who were bizarrely joint captains and both sporting an armband each. Banks won the coin toss and spotted the ball on the centre circle. Tommy sat on the grass near De Boat, Case and Dwops. Banks kicked off. Kling took off down the wing, stepping past a small boy who seemed to have put his boots on the wrong feet. The boy swung wildly at the ball as Kling tapped it through his legs. His momentum made him spin around in a circle and fall over in a heap. Some of the crowd laughed as Kling continued towards the Hawksmoor penalty area. Banks was screaming for Kling to pass it back to him as he also approached the Hawksmoor goal. Kling looked up and chipped the ball over the head of Ronny Thompson, aiming for Banks on the back post. The ball hung in the air as Banks shaped up, ready to volley it, but suddenly Bailey appeared, jumping high, heading the ball up and over the Hawksmoor keeper.

One-nil to Ridgeway.

'Yes!' Tommy cheered, punching the air.

Banks was still scowling as Ronny Thompson took the centre. His twin brother was on the left wing and Ron pinged the ball straight to him. Riley trapped the ball and pinged it back towards Ronny who had started running down the right. Banks tried to intercept the ball, but as soon as it got to Ronny it was launched quickly back the other way to Riley, who had run past Kling and was now in front of Ally. Ally stepped towards him, but the same thing happened, and the ball flew back across the pitch in behind Harry where Ronny Thompson was waiting to volley the ball past Big Mac.

One-all.

Tommy pulled Alf's card out of his sock, careful to ensure no one was looking.

'What's the score?' Tommy mouthed silently.

'Nil-nil,' Alf mouthed back.

As it stood, Ridgeway would need to win by three clear goals. Tommy stashed Alf back in his sock and turned his attention back to the game. Bailey had possession of the ball and was striding down the centre of the pitch with Riley and Ronny chasing her. Banks was shouting at her to pass to him and so was Kling, but instead, she clipped it into Leon. Mee caught the ball on his thigh and dropped it to the floor. A big sandy-haired boy ran straight into him and knocked him over.

Mr Point blew the whistle. 'Free kick.'

Bailey had picked up the ball, but Banks snatched it off her.

'Are you stupid, Scott? I take the free kicks,' he snarled. Bailey put her hands up and walked away. Banks spotted the ball as Mr Point walked the Hawksmoor wall that consisted of both the Thompsons and the small spinning lad, Arthur Sleep, back the customary ten yards. When the wall was set, Mr Point blew his whistle again and Banks drilled the ball straight at the small lad on the end of the wall. Arthur instinctively dived to the floor and the ball sailed over him and straight into the net past the Hawksmoor keeper, who had not expected his wall to disintegrate. Banks tore off down the wing with his shirt over his head, narrowly missing running into Mrs Mee, who was arguing with the mum of the big sandy-haired boy. Tommy was just glad she didn't have her umbrella.

Two-one.

Two more needed.

The game ebbed and flowed with both teams going close but neither managing to score. Tommy had checked

169

in with Alf several times and it remained nil-nil at Old Green. Tommy was just putting Alf back in his sock when he noticed the crowd getting excited. He looked up to see Ronny Thompson dribbling at Harry, Bailey in hot pursuit. Just as Harry got close, he switched the play instinctively, knowing that his twin would be expecting it. Sure enough, Riley sped past Kling and trapped the ball in mid-air. Ally stepped in his way, but Riley calmly stepped over the ball, feinting to go inside but actually going outside of the now-stranded Gayter. Riley was poised to strike on his left foot, but Banks ran across him to block the shot, so instead he switched the ball across the box to where Ron was waiting to shoot. He hit the ball first time, low to Mackenzie's right. Mac dived quickly and tipped the ball wide of the post, but it dropped straight in front of Riley, who calmly chipped the ball into the exposed right corner.

Two-two: halftime.

Mr Point crouched down with his tactics board and started giving out instructions, including switching Bailey and Harry for Wayne and Rohan. Tommy slowly shook his head as he caught his friends' eyes. Banks was moved into his usual central midfield slot and Dwops on the left. With three goals now needed, winning the league was looking highly unlikely.

The two teams went back onto the pitch and Hawksmoor took the centre. Leon pressed quickly but Riley just flicked the ball to Ronny who then ran at Banks. Banks slide-tackled him hard and Ron went down heavily.

'Play on!' called out Mr Point as Banks regained the ball and started to advance towards the Hawksmoor goal.

The Hawksmoor parents were protesting in vain. Riley clearly didn't like the way Banks had hurt his brother and he started to chase after him. Si Kling was on the right, calling for the ball, Leon was peeling off to the left, but Banks was all about himself, he had no intention of passing. The big sandy-haired boy ran towards Banks, which slowed him up just enough for Riley to arrive and scythe Banks down from behind.

'Arrrgh!' Banks cried out. Mr Point blew his whistle and announced the free kick. He crouched down by Banks and started shaking his head. Robin's dad ran on and crouched down on his other side. The two men lifted a sobbing Banks off the pitch, just as Leon's mum started swinging her handbag around her head like an Olympic hammer thrower. She was gesticulating franticly at a tall thin woman Tommy guessed was Mrs Thompson. Leon's dad and a tall man in a tracksuit were making a barrier in between them.

'Tommy, you're on,' Mr Point called over.

Harry took off his shirt and passed it to Tommy. 'Here you go, mate,' he said as he passed it over.

Tommy pulled the shirt over his head and tucked a handful of fabric into the waistband of his oversized shorts. Leon Mee was standing over the free kick and Mr Point was having a word with Riley Thompson. Ronny, who was back on his feet, was standing next to his brother pointing at where Banks had clattered into him.

'This is your chance, Tommy,' a voice called over from the crowd as he stepped over the white line.

Tommy looked over to see Mr Nomos, broom still in his hand. Tommy nodded just as his feet started to tingle. They were making him walk towards the edge of the penalty area like an octopus-controlled marionette. Leon looked over at him and nodded. Because of Tommy's size, other players didn't really consider him a threat and so he was only being marked by little Arthur Sleep. Mr Point blew the whistle and Leon chipped the ball over the Thompson twin wall towards Tommy. The boots started to tingle more. Tommy followed their lead and stepped in front of Sleep. The ball dropped down to around Tommy's stomach height. Suddenly, his left boot swung up and he volleyed the ball sweetly towards the goal. The Hawksmoor keeper just managed to get a hand to it to deflect the ball onto the crossbar. The ball ricocheted towards Wayne Dwops. Dwops looked horrified that the ball was at his feet and instinctively kicked the ball away like it was about to explode. Luckily for Ridgeway, it flew into the roof of the net. Si Kling jumped on Dwops in celebration and the two boys fell over in a heap. Leon jumped on next then De Boat and Ally. Big Mac was thundering up the pitch from goal. Tommy could only see Wayne's feet sticking out of the impromptu pile-on and they had already stopped wriggling. Tommy couldn't look. Mac threw himself right on the top of the stack and a sound like badly played bagpipes ensued from the mass of arms and legs.

'Gerroff, Mac!' Mee called out from the six-boy huddle. The pile slowly unravelled one boy at a time until only Wayne was left.

'Urrrrrggghhh!' Wayne did not look good.

'Bailey, switch with Wayne, please,' Mr Point called out.

Three-two: Ridgeway

Riley spotted the ball and play resumed. Ronny ran past Kling and looked to switch the play again. Bailey wasn't falling for it this time and tracked Riley down the other wing. As the ball came over, she intercepted it and passed it back to Mac. Mac saw Leon high up the pitch and thumped it straight to him. Tommy's feet started to tingle, and they made him run past Mee. Big Sandy-hair tried to tackle Leon, but Leon just calmly tapped it though his long legs. Next was Mr Sleep, but instead of trying to take him on, he passed the ball to Tommy. Tommy had just the keeper to beat but the boots stopped working, taking Tommy completely by surprise. He froze for a split second, unsure of what to do next as he had been relying on the autopilot.

'Go on, Tommy,' Leon called out.

Tommy snapped back into focus. Glancing over his shoulder, he could see the Thompson twins racing towards him. *Okay, okay, I can do this*, he thought to himself. The keeper was edging towards the near post, which left the far post as the biggest target. Shoot across the keeper, his dad had always told him. Make the keeper work, he would say. Tommy pushed the ball half a step in front of him, then struck the ball with the outside of his right foot, slicing the outside of the ball, making it spin viciously in the air. The banana shot, his dad had called it when they'd seen players do it on the TV. The ball curled in a perfect arc around the keeper and nestled in the top corner.

Four-two.

Bailey was the first to him, wrapping her arms around him and kissing him on the cheek.

'Great goal, Tommy,' she said in his ear. Leon arrived next, but Tommy put his hands up as he got closer.

'Don't worry I'm not gonna kiss yer,' Mee laughed. Instead, he just put out his fist for Tommy to bump. 'Good goal, buddy.'

Tommy could feel his cheeks burning as he made his way back to his own half joyous; he had scored but was equally embarrassed that everyone had just seen him get a kiss from a girl on a football pitch. Okay, professional players kissed each other all the time, but this was different. Tommy looked over at Harry, who was still clapping his best mate.

'Get in there, Tommy,' he shouted across. Tommy beamed back at him. Ronny Thompson put the ball on the spot. It was obvious who he would pass to, and Tommy didn't need the boots to tell him what to do. He started running across towards Riley's side and, sure enough, Ronny kicked the ball to his brother. Tommy was straight onto Riley as he brought the ball under control. Riley stepped over the ball, attempting

173

another feint, but Tommy read the dummy and whipped the ball off Riley's foot. Tommy was off. He ran past Riley and attacked down the left wing. Hawksmoor also had a girl playing for them. Tommy knew her from the park matches in the holidays – Ayla White. She was in year five, the same as Bailey, but she wasn't as good as her. Still, Tommy knew he had to give her respect because she was still better than most of the year five boys Tommy knew. Ayla came in at him sideways on, which was making it difficult for him to take her on.

'Tommy!' Bailey called.

Tommy looked up and saw Bailey in space. He passed the ball just in front of her, so she didn't need to break stride, and she accelerated with the ball straight towards the sandy-haired giant. 'One, two,' she called out towards Leon, passing the ball into his feet. She ran around the opposite side of the sandy mountain and Leon passed it back to her. Arthur tried to block her path, but Bailey just rainbow-flicked the ball over his head. The poor lad tried to turn quickly to see where the ball had gone, but got his laces tangled and he fell to the floor. Just the keeper to beat. He rushed out to close the space, but Bailey calmly dragged the ball back with her right sole, let the ball run backwards behind her left leg, then quickly scooped the ball with the inside of her right foot round the back of her standing foot and used her laces to push the ball forward through the keeper's open legs in one fluid move. The Hocus Pocus move. The stuff of legends. Even Robin Banks couldn't do it. Tommy knew this because at lunchtime he would see him practising with Owen Cash, both saying it was impossible. Well, it wasn't because Bailey had just done it. Not only that, but she had also scored with it. Tommy looked over to see if Banks was watching but it looked like he had gone. Instead, Tommy saw a familiar red lampshade of a hat. Mr Rees waved over at Tommy, so Tommy waved back, suddenly conscious that if he was the only one who could see Mr Ree it would look very odd that he was waving. Sure enough, a group of giggling girls started waving back at him, Amber Dextrous right in the middle of them using both hands. Tommy put his hand on his forehead. He had only just got his drawer back to normal, Bailey agreeing that four months later was an okay time to put old love letters in the bin. Bailey was celebrating with Ally and Leon. She looked over a little crestfallen that Tommy hadn't come over to congratulate her and now it was her turn to blush. Tommy started to walk over to her, but she ran back into her own half ready for the restart.

Five-two.

If the score stayed like this, Ridgeway would win the league. Or would they? In all the excitement of playing, Tommy hadn't been able to check in with Alf.

'Mr P, I need to do my laces,' Tommy lied. He crouched down and pulled Alf's card out of his sock discreetly. Alf had a serious face on. 'What's the score?' Tommy asked.

'One-nil to All Saints. Jack Pott scored,' Alf said glumly.

Tommy sighed and stashed Alf back in his sock. Well, that was it then, Tommy thought. They'd tried but they were never going to able to influence the Old Green game. *I might as well just enjoy the rest of this one,* he thought to himself.

'Are you ready, Tommy?' Mr P called over.

'Yes, sir,' Tommy replied. Mr P blew the whistle and Tommy ran towards Riley again. This time, though, Ronny pinged the ball hard at Kling's legs. The ball bounced off his shins, straight back to Ron's feet, who then set off at pace towards Ally and Rohan. Instead of aiming for one of them, he ran towards the centre, bringing them both into play. Both boys rushed out to sandwich him. Riley had made an overlapping run behind Ronny, who back-heeled the ball straight to his twin without looking. Riley sprinted past De

Boat and into the space he had left behind him after being drawn into the middle. Riley had a clear shot at goal, and he took it. Fortunately, the ball went straight towards Mac, who caught it cleanly. Ally drifted wide and Mac threw the ball to his feet. Ayla White closed him down but wasn't quick enough to stop a Gayter special being launched right up the other end. Bailey headed the ball back towards Tommy, who jinked past Sleep, using his low centre of gravity to spin him like a top. The poor lad would need a bucket soon! Next up was the sandy-haired giant who, due to his height, was quite slow. Tommy flip-flapped the ball one way then quickly sole-rolled the ball back towards the big lad. A huge foot planted itself near the ball, but Tommy had caused him to stretch his legs wide, perfect for an easy Panna. Tommy continued his maze-like run towards the keeper, who was more cautious this time after what Bailey had done to him.

'Tommy!' Leon called out.

Tommy saw Leon running into the penalty area on his left. Following Mr Nomos's advice, Tommy set the ball brilliantly on a plate for Leon to run onto and smash it past the Hawksmoor keeper.

'Pass and move, pass and move!' Mr Nomos cheered.

Tommy caught his eye and smiled.

Six-two.

And that's the way it finished. Whilst the players were shaking hands, Tommy ran to the pavilion and fished Alf from his hiding place.

'Well?' Tommy asked impatiently, but Alf wasn't there. 'Alf, Alf, where are you?' Tommy stared at the empty card for a minute, just as Harry entered the pavilion.

'Why are you hiding in here, Tommy?' Harry asked.

'Er, no reason,' Tommy stammered. 'I was just gonna get changed quickly.'

'Well, you're missing all the fun, mate, come on, you can

get changed later, and anyways, this bloke is looking for you.'

'Bloke?' Tommy asked, curiosity on his face.

'Just hurry up,' Harry said as he left.

Tommy was just about to put Alf back in his sock when Alf appeared, red-faced and out of breath.

'What was the final score, Alf?' Tommy demanded.

'Give me a minute, lad,' Alf puffed. 'Now, what was it?'

'Oh, come on, Alf, please don't joke,' Tommy implored him.

'Okay, okay. Well, it didn't finish one-nil, it was…' Alf paused for dramatic effect.

'Why you-a teez eem, Alf? Tommy, it wossa one eeech.' Toni had come into the frame with a big smile on his face. 'Tu, hee a score right at da fineesh.'

'That means we've won the league on goal difference,' Tommy said excitedly.

'Well done, lad,' Alf congratulated.

'Congratulazioni, Tommy,' Toni agreed.

Tommy stashed Alf's card back in his sock, intrigued as to who the bloke was that was looking for him. Could Harry now see Mr Ree? He knew Bailey had spotted him, but she was far more observant than Harry and no one else had ever mentioned him. Which was odd because Mr Ree didn't look like your average spectator. Tommy went back outside to investigate. Players and parents were all milling around talking, as Mr Point tidied away the nets. Tommy looked for Mr Ree, but he was nowhere to be seen. He spotted Bailey and Harry standing next to Bailey's dad and a tall man in a tracksuit, so he wandered over. As he made his way through the people dotted about, the big sandy-haired boy appeared and put out a huge hand. 'Good game, Tommy,' he said. 'I'm Guy, Guy Lyath. You were the best player on the pitch today.'

'Thanks,' Tommy said shaking his hand.

'Tommy, there you are, there is someone I would like you to meet,' Mr Scott interrupted as he approached. 'Tommy, this is Dave, we used to play together at the Blues academy.'

'Hi, Tommy,' Dave said, offering his hand to shake. 'I thought you did really well out there today.'

'Tommy, Dave now scouts for the Reds and wondered if you would like to try out next year when the new season starts. I told him you probably wouldn't, being such a big Blues fan and all.' Mr Scott laughed.

Tommy's jaw hit the floor. Was this really happening?

'That's right, Tommy, so what do you think?' Dave asked. 'Obviously, I will need to speak to your mum and give her all the details, but you are just the sort of player I am looking for: small, low centre of balance and good spatial awareness. You have some bad habits and an unusual running style at times, but we can work on that.'

Tommy was nodding his head quickly, still speechless. *He wants me because I'm small.* Harry came over and patted him on the back.

'Wow, Tommy, this is what you've always wanted,' his friend said grinning.

Tommy's smile was so big it was hurting him. He looked over to see where Bailey was, but she'd gone.

Tommy and Harry were walking home, bags slung over their shoulders.

'I wonder how Old Green got on tonight, Tom?' Harry mused. 'Do you think they could have won?'

'Not sure,' Tommy lied. 'Let's hope so, although a draw would do it.'

'Yeah, fingers crossed,' Harry agreed. 'How good was Bailey's header, though?'

Bailey. Things had been awkward since she had scored her second goal and he'd not celebrated with her.

'Tom?' Harry quizzed again.

'Er, yeah, but her second was the best, surely? She did

178

the Hocus Pocus and scored!' Tommy marvelled again as he replayed the scene in his head.

'Oh yeah, I bet Banks was fuming!' Harry chuckled, also aware of how many lunchtimes Banks had spent practising it.

'Not sure he saw it, Haz, his dad had taken him home.'

'It might be bad then,' Harry said.

'Yeah, maybe.' Tommy felt guilty about his wish that Banks would break his leg.

The boys had started to walk a little bit quicker, each trying to edge ahead as the corner of Granville Street appeared. Tommy allowed Harry a little head start as the taller boy broke into a sprint, then he tore after him. Closing the gap quickly, he kept within touching distance as they passed the second lamppost, but then Tommy started to slow down just a little as he let his best friend win for the first time.

'Yes, yes, it's gold for Smith!' Harry was jumping and whooping with his arms aloft. Harry mimed taking something off and over his head and then handed it to Tommy. 'Here you go.'

'What is it?' Tommy asked.

'Silver!' Harry chuckled, and he raced up to his gate, still jumping and whooping. 'See you tomorrow, Tom,' he shouted over his shoulder.

Tommy smiled as he opened the door and went inside.

'Hey, Mum,' he called out.

'Hiya, pet,' she replied. 'Dinner will be ready in half an hour.'

'Okay, I'm just going to pop out on my bike then.'

'Half an hour, pet, don't be late.'

Tommy rode over to Old Green and collected Toni's card from the big oak tree. As he turned into Maurice Road, he could see Mr Ree's shop at the top. He rode up to the door and propped his bike against the window. The small bell chimed above him as he pushed the door open into the store. Tommy closed the door and was amazed to see that all the shelves were empty. He looked at the main counter at the back of the shop and saw the familiar small old man in his fawn-coloured overalls and red hat.

'Hello, Tommy,' said Mr Ree. 'You played well today.'

'Thank you,' Tommy replied. 'Mr Ree, why are all the shelves empty?'

'Because it's moving day. Have you brought your boots back?' Mr Ree asked.

'Er, no,' Tommy said. 'I thought I could keep them.'

'Tommy, have you not realised? You do not need them anymore. When you have magic feet, why would you ever need magic boots?'

Tommy thought he understood what Mr Ree meant about magic feet, although he should probably cut his toenails. 'Where are you moving to?' Tommy asked.

'I'm not sure yet, Tommy, I am waiting for my next assignment. Now, let's see about those boots, shall we?' he said. Mr Ree picked up the thin silver whistle that was on the counter and blew into it again and yet still it made no sound that Tommy could hear. He put the whistle down and laced his fingers on top of the counter, slowly twisting his thumbs over and over each other. After a few seconds, the curtain behind Mr Ree moved and the box that Tommy recognised was pushed up on top of the counter with the same little hands either side of it. The curtain moved again and Mr Ree opened the box with Stan's boots in. He picked one up and turned it over and then put it back in the box, placing it under the counter. Suddenly, the curtain twitched again, and the little hands slid another little box that Tommy didn't recognise onto the counter.

'Thank you, Clive,' Mr Ree said.

'Clive? I thought his name was Kevin?' Tommy enquired.

'Don't be silly, Tommy, Kevin doesn't work on Wednesdays.' Mr Ree pushed the much newer-looking box towards Tommy. 'Here you go, these are for you.'

Tommy opened the box, lifting the lid carefully and revealing a pair of brand new, shiny white boots with a green insignia on the side. On top of them there was a folded piece of paper. Tommy picked it up and looked at the writing inside, which simply said:

Green, get it? X

'But...' Tommy began, tears in his eyes.

'Tommy, if people just accepted that they do not need to know all the answers and took more time to just appreciate the wonders around them...'

'The world would be a more magical place,' Tommy finished.

'Exactly,' Mr Ree said, picking up a clipboard and pen, crossing something out. 'Ah yes now, the cards, Tommy, do you have them, please?'

Tommy fished the cards out of his pocket.

'I will leave you to say goodbye,' Mr Ree said, and he turned and went behind the thick purple curtain.

Tommy looked down at the smiling Alf and Toni.

'Hey, guys, I guess this is goodbye,' Tommy said.

'It has been a pleasure to meet you, lad,' Alf replied.

'Arrivederci e buona fortuna,' Toni nodded. 'I wheel miss you, Tomee.'

'Thank you for all your help. Will I ever see you again?' Tommy asked.

'Who knows, lad, but although you might not see us, we will still see you.'

Mr Ree returned with the old green tobacco tin. He

opened it carefully and put Alf and Toni back inside with the other old football cards, binding them altogether with the thick rubber band. He put the tin on the counter and then held out his hand.

'It has been an adventure, Tommy.'

Tommy shook Mr Ree's hand.

'Thank you,' Tommy said. 'For everything.'

'You are most welcome, Tommy. Now we should really be getting you home, I think your dinner is ready.'

Tommy tucked the new shoe box under one arm and followed Mr Ree down one of the corridors of empty shelves, eventually coming to a door. Mr Ree opened it and stepped to one side as usual. Tommy stepped out onto Maurice Road. His bike was propped up against the fence near a small garden gate. He turned back to say goodbye to Mr Ree but the back door of the shop had been replaced and was now a door that Tommy recognised. It opened slowly and an old lady peered out.

'Can I help you, love?' she asked.

'Um, no, I'm okay, thank you,' Tommy answered.

'Oh, it's you again,' the old lady said. 'I've already told you it's not nice to pick on the elderly, now clear off.'

'But...'

The old lady disappeared and returned with a broom.

'Go on, get!' she said as she started sweeping it towards him.

Tommy didn't need to be told twice; he raced to his bike and sped home, new boots under his arm. After his dinner, Tommy talked his mum through a complete play by play of the game. He had spent most of it trying to explain the Hocus Pocus move and the scout who had said he could trial for the Reds next season. He went up to his room with mixed feelings of guilt and joy in his stomach.

~~I hate Robin Banks.~~ I hope Banks has not broken his leg. Bailey scored a Hocus Pocus today, it was awesome. But not as awesome as when she kissed me. Does this mean she likes me? I thought she liked Neil Downe. I think she is cross with me, though. ☹ Mr Ree is moving away, I will miss him, and Toni and Alf. He gave me some new boots, though, which I think are from my dad. Not sure how that is even possible, but I have learnt not to question it. It is just great to know he is watching me from somewhere. I love you, Dad.

Tommy finished his diary entry with a picture of Bailey scoring her wonder goal and stashed it back under his mattress. He went to sleep with his new boots on and his note from his dad under his pillow.

Final Whistle

Tommy arrived at school early and made his way to the sports board. The final table was up and so was a little cut-out picture of the World Cup with a handwritten sign that said Ridgeway were the league winners.

Mr Point may not be the best coach in the world, but Tommy loved him for all the effort he put in to make football that bit more special for them all. Although Tommy knew that Ridgeway had won, he hadn't told a soul, not even his mum. Tommy studied the league table. It had been such a close run thing, just a two goal difference separating Ridgeway and All Saints. Tommy hated to admit it, but next season would be a lot harder without Banks and the other GO6L lads. Who was going to play in goal?

League Table

	W	D	L	Pts	F	A	GD
Ridgeway	3	1	1	10	21	12	+9
All Saints	3	1	1	10	23	16	+7
Lawton	2	3	0	9	23	19	+4
Thornside	2	2	1	8	12	14	-2
Old Green	0	2	3	1	12	17	-5
Hawksmoor	0	1	4	1	10	23	-13

Top Goal Scorers

James Nasium (Lawton) 18

Jack Pott (All Saints) 14

Jaun Tu (Old Green) 11

David Jones (All Saints) 6

Robin Banks (Ridgeway) 6

Markus Absent (Thornside) 5

Leon Mee (Ridgeway) 5

Riley Thompson (Hawksmoor) 5

Ronny Thompson (Hawksmoor) 5

Daniel Williams (Lawton) 4

Ray Deo (All Saints) 3

Bailey Scott (Ridgeway) 3

Mike Raphone (Thornside) 2

Robert Smyth (Thornside) 2

Simon Kling (Ridgeway) 2

Owen Cash (Ridgeway) 2

Thomas Green (Ridgeway) 2

Diego Ortiz (Lawton) 1

Orson Kart (Thornside) 1

Rick O'Shea (Thornside) 1

Neil Downe (Thornside) 1

Wayne Dwops (Ridgeway) 1

Tommy was looking at the scorer's list as Harry and Bailey rounded the corner and ran over to the board. He hoped things would not be awkward with Bailey today after the kiss. Tommy had been so surprised, instead of doing the robot, he'd just stood there doing a mannequin challenge instead.

'Did we win?' Bailey asked impatiently.

'Yeah, on goal difference, All Saints drew one-all,' Tommy said.

'Get in!' Harry said, high-fiving Tommy.

Tommy looked at Bailey as she studied the stats on the board.

'We okay?' Tommy asked.

Bailey looked at him and Harry and pulled both boys into a tight group hug.

'Of course, because we are The Three Amigos, and the new league winners.'

'Yeah we are!' Tommy beamed.

The three friends started to jump up and down, singing, 'Championees, championees, are we, are we, are we!'

Epilogue

That afternoon, Tommy sat in class WD4T looking out of the window at the grass. What a year it had been. Tommy had dreamed of the day for so long that he would get to score in the red-and-black school nets and be asked to trial at a professional club. Last night his dreams had come true, scoring for school at home and being scouted for the Reds for next season. Then there was Mr Ree and his shop, Stan's old boots and Alf and Toni. It was quite unbelievable when you stopped and thought about it, but now he understood why his dad always said: 'Football is magic, Tommy.'

To be continued...